CLEOPATRA
QUEEN OF EXILE
by
R. David Simpson

Dedication

DEDICATED TO MY FIRST DAUGHTER, LISA

Table of Contents

3

Information

Cleopatra VII - Queen of Egypt . Time frames for this story:

Age18– 51 BC. Becomes Queen, co-ruler.(father dies)

Age 19 - 50 BC. Queen with her brother as King.

Age 20 - 49 BC. Queen with her brother as King.

Age 21 - 48 BC. Escapes to Syria.

Age 22 –47 BC.- Still in Syria. Age 23 - She returns to Egypt.

Age 23- 46 BC. - Honeymoon on the Nile.

Cleopatra's Entourage:

Applodorus - Loyal male Servant. (2)Diogenes -Advisor, languages and medicine.

(3) Jahi - Advisor, tutor to Cleopatra on military matters. (4) Charmion-friend and maid-in-waiting . (5) Iras -friend and maid-in-waiting

Her Palace Adversaries:

(1) Arsinoë IV - Cleopatra's younger sister (2) Ptolemy XII King of Egypt - Her brother-husband. (3) Achilles   - Advisor & Head of the army Phothinius -Political advisor

Other Players: (1) Bibulus - Governor of Syria under the command of Pompey.

(2)King Azar - Syrian Arab king of many nomadic tribes Ekmet

Cleopatra's Royal Guard Leader Royal Guards- All female guards.

Julius Caesar - Dictator of Rome, 'Husband' to Cleopatra

General Anthony - Right-hand man to Caesar

General Tullius -   General to Caesar General

General Servius - General to Caesar.

General Sapinus - General to Caesar.

Roman Senate House Speaker- Young Ceriro

Aglea, Dareia, Evgenia -The Three Oligarchy, wealthy Greek women.

Based on the Script 'Cleopatra, Queen of Exile'

46 BC. Summer, Alexandria City, The Royal Docks.

From darkness, Africa came into the light, and as the new day's orb shone on the African continent, Egypt's Alexandria City awoke to the heat and smells of a new days' life. The dawn's early grey light, reflects off the calm Nile waters and as the sun peaks over the horizon, casting grey then pink light upon the Pyramids. Slowly life comes back to a new day. Small frogs croaked from the muddy reeds, alligators peek out from the Nile River and blink in the new sunlight. The ancient city of Alexandria, now 300 years old, greets fishermen coming back for breakfast with their morning catch.

Near the Alexandrian Palace, servants scurried here and there, collecting and packing silver plates, gold, glass cups along with jugs of beer, cheese and wine.

Fragrances of morimga oil, nard oil lemon-grass, frankincense, myrrh, marjoram, henna hair dye from Cyprus, rose from containers to be placed in Cleopatra's bedroom on her ship, along with mirrors of Egyptian glass, combs of sandalwood, jewelry of string of pearls and matching earrings and dresses for Cleopatra to choose each day of the two month trip. All carefully packed into containers and carried outside. Baskets of barley, honey in blue glass jars, dried beef, perch fish, dried mutton, vegetables of onions, beans, turnips, lettuce and more, all for the oarsmen, the servants and the guests.

The Grand, Royal Barge is tied up at the Royal Docks and in the process of being loaded by hundreds of half-naked, sweating, women, who skillfully carry boxes on their heads and onto the barge, carefully placed below in the bedrooms, kitchen and bathing pool, on the lower deck. Nearby, at the Isis temple, the priests offer thanks and incense to the newly wedded couple, who are about to embark on their honeymoon. A wedding trip, recognized by Egypt, but not in Rome.

Two nobles watch from the ship's rail, watching the sunrise in the morning sky. Cleopatra, almost twenty-two years of age, clad in beautiful long white hand woven translucent linen. She wore the Royal triple snaked head crown upon her young head, the only triple crown ever used. She has the look of a Queen and a new wife . She now is, officially recognized by Caesar, the late Ruler of Rome as the rightful Queen of Egypt. Her bothersome brother was now dead, her sister locked up on Ephesus Island near Greece. She gave no thought to the fact that Caesar demanded she marries her other younger brother to show to the common Egyptians. She knew that no one was fooled by that political arrangement, but it had to be done to please the commoners, who would otherwise worry that a female leader ruling on her own would not be strong enough to satisfy the gods. Caesar stood beside her, now the Roman Empire's leader, at fifty-two years of age. His patrician countenance marred by decades of scars. He also understood that he had finally reached his goal of being just as great as 'Alexandria the Great' and uniting with Cleopatra, binds him as close as he can ever be, with that great man, his long, dead idol.

They nibbled on dates, dark Syrian figs and ripe plums, as servants labored below. Cleopatra, teasingly, started a new conversation as the ship left the dock for the Upper Nile tour. "My husband, what happened in with you while in Gaul?" Caesar cleared his mouth of food and replied. "Ah yes, my Cleo, that is a long, long story". He took a swig of wine and began. "We had just completed conquering those northern Gauls and were just about to do the same to that cold, wet rock, we now call Britannica". Caesar rubbed his near balding head and thought back to those nine rough years in Europe before coming to Egypt.

"Yes, he said, I remember. It all started when I first heard about these the chance of borrowing money from three Greek oligarch's wives. I needed money to raise my own army. I was told that the elder fat one, Aglea, the thin Dareia, and the old one, Evgengia, sat in the steam rooms, almost naked amidst the steam, talking about me as though they that they, like men, controlled Rome. From what my intermediary told me, the women said, "We can control these Romans and the empire if Caesar remains cooperative". Dareia,

"I think he will continue to cooperate, he so yearns to be another 'Alexander the Great', ha, and he will be well into debt!". Evgenia said, "So, let us send him our orders and tell him to return to Rome and take care of Pompey as soon as he gets Europe under control". Aglea smiled, "Then let it be done."

I was warned by my friends about 'Greeks bearing gifts' but, well, when hearing what the women said about me, I decided to take their money, and see who controls who in the end. I then called up my army then marched out from Italy towards Gaul. Being ordered by the Senate to quell the Gauls that had been attacking their allies in the south of Gaul. I decided to take matters into my own hands and moved all the way to the shores of Britannica, unknown territory and feared by many for its ghosts and strange blue people. That was all nine years ago when you were still a young woman and not yet sovereign."

54-51 BC. Britannica and Gaul.

Caesar could see from his ship's castle, a young girl, playing near the shoreline. The vessel had just slipped out of a fog, suddenly she looked up and saw us and with a fright ran away. He could hear her cry out, "Look, ships, strange ships!" 'Two older women, cleaning fish on the beach, looked up in surprise and looked out to sea. The oldest woman cried out in alarm, "Run to the cliffs"!

Soon, the Roman ships hit the beach, thousands of Romans pouring out into the shallow water. Out of one Caesar came and hit the water, surrounded by his men. Quickly he thrust a flag into the sand and said "I, Julius Caesar, in the name of Rome claim this land!" Antony, his closest friend and general, looked up to see the Celts lining the cliff top, shouting insults to come and fight.

Antony shouted back to his men, "Line up men, prepare to fight. We have company. "Let's move!"

But they did not move. The Romans hesitated. They were afraid for the first time in many years, of this mysterious fog-drenched island, of its evil spirits. Above, on the cliffs, the Celtic warriors had gathered. They chanted an ancient song, loudly challenging his troops. Caesar came forward and spoke loudly, facing his men. "I Am just a man, like you, and I do not fear this island. Do you, my mighty Romans, have fear? You, the conquerors of Gaul? You have nothing to fear but fear itself. Will you not follow me? "

He moved forward off the beach. His men look at him and, were suddenly ashamed, and with one voice shouted, "Yes! All victory to Rome! "All victory to our Caesar and Jupiter' and charged forward off the ships. Above the beach, hundreds of blue-faced men gathering with bows at the ready. As the Romans headed up the cliff paths, the Celts release their arrows.

But it's hard to hit anyone, the cliffs were too steep, none of his men can really be seen until they hit the tops of the paths. Then the real fighting started. Bare-chested Celts attacked heavily armored Romans, many of each side falling over the cliffs, close-range arrows bounced off armor or stuck into Roman eyes. Celtic tribesmen fell like wounded blades of grass, with cut legs, slashed ribs, punctured lungs. As more Romans came to the top, more Celts died, and it's soon all over. The wounded Celts were rounded up. His troops pushed inland seeking women and children and to prepared to make camp."

Caesar looked at the captured and ordered a soldier to take some men and younger captives and see if they could find any pearl shells in these waters nearby. Rumor had it that these waters are full of pearls. The soldier smiled, saluted and snapped off a "Yes, Sire". I'll tie some children to the boats and send them down".

Caesar replied, "Alright, but be sure to spare the women and children injury, we need them as healthy slaves".

As rain clouds formed, his troops started mopping up, herding prisoners onto ships, killing others and preparing to leave for Gaul. Huts were burned, women cried, and children screamed at the horror that is war. Caesar, Antony, and his generals walked through the mud near their camp. As he did, he said, "Make sure you save the younger women for our men. Cut the hands off the farmers who resisted giving food and neck-slice the wounded. Board the rest as slaves". Nearby, General Tullius, now old at forty-five, a gruff veteran of this kind of thing said, "I'll see to it".

Caesar, looking at his generals, "This time, we have defeated two enemies, our men fear of this island, and we've made a permanent mark on these blue devils". Sapinus, the oldest of his generals, at fifty, stated, " Yes, but having come so far to take so little from this rock, we had better reward the men soon". Caesar looked at him and replied, The men shall have their pick of the Celtic women and our backers, friends will have our pick of thousands of Gallic slaves. That should keep them happy". Sapinus looked about and commented, "Piss of an island anyway, this place. Wouldn't grow a decent grape!" he said, as he spat on the wet ground.

Later, he saw a strange captive and stopped to ask "Who might this long-haired mongrel be?" The soldier saluted and stated, "Caesar, he's the Druid high priest of these people. They read the fortunes of men, it is said". Caesar asked, rather mockingly to the prisoner, "Is that right? You read the fortunes of men? So, what is my fortune, pray to tell?" The Captive, a Druid leader, took Caesars' hand and looks carefully at it and spoke in Gaelic. The soldier being Gaelic, translated for him. "The gods predict you shall be a great warrior and your son divine. You will do well until the seventh year, the third month of your reign as king. Then, you shall die as you deserve". The Druid Leader spat on the ground. Caesar was shocked at his manner and statement mockingly replied, "Ah, my friend, divine sons, possibly, but there are no kings in my country. You are wrong. Soldier, crucify him along with Cassivellaunus "The soldier saluted and snapped off a quick, "Yes, Sire!" And that was the end of that silly prediction.

That night, Antony and other generals reclined and went over the day's events. Torchlights flickers near the guards at the door, servants checked paperwork. Caesar sat at his field desk and wrote his history as he was want to do as he moved through Europe and then started on a letter to the young Egyptian Princess, Cleopatra.

The Druids were people that fascinated Caesar. His men, who at first was afraid to even get out of their ships and fight these people Island people. Behind all these strange nude fighting men and women were these Druids. Their history is cloaked in mystery. The ancient Druids were members a revered social status among the Celts due to their

9

service to the community as priests and teachers. These priests were venerated as were the oak tree and the dead. They believe in the immortality of the soul, that is why they are not afraid to die. They think they are coming back, soon in another life! Caesar had heard that these Druids were affecting the Gauls so thought, they have to deal with them first if he was to win over these people.

Antony, drinking wine nearby commented with his usual dry humor asked me, "Writing to that fifteen-year-old Egyptian wench again?" Caesar replied, "Keeping in touch with a future queen will make it easier when the time comes to take possession of Egypt, of course". Antony persisted and asked "And, pray tell, what have you written", as he read over Caesar's shoulder. Antony read, somewhat mockingly.

'Dear Cleopatra', I have come to the end of the known world and conquered these blue barbarians. Now it is back to Gaul. Happy birthday to you with gifts from Gaul. When next you write, I would be pleased if you referred to me as 'Uncle".

Antony smiled and commented ,"All sounds very cosy. Now, what about Gaul? We have gone too far north. The Senate is after your neck."

Caesar continued to write, not looking up and stated "I'm more worried about the plebs and my image. What I've conquered needs to be told to the plebs first."

Antony, always on his toes quipped "The slaves we take back plus a good campaign slogan will do it". Finally, Caesar paid attention, looked up and asked "Like what?". Tullius, standing nearby, piped in. "Well", he said as he gestured with his hands, "How about something to the point, like, 'I came, I saw, I conquered!" Caesar thought about that and stated, "Ha, yes, that has as a good ring to it, I'll use it." Then, looking at the scribe slave, said, "Have the pigeons released with Cleopatra's letter and the tidings of good news". And with that ended the night with, "Let us set sail for Portus Itius."

Caesar headed southward into Gaul towards Italy, his mighty army clashed with the last of the Treveri fighters who have refused to surrender to Roman occupation and orders. Caesar and his generals, watched from the high ground, on horseback, near the riverbank of the mighty Rhine River. Caesar ordered General Sapinus, to move the cavalry in from the left and right flanks. Stating, "let us settle this fight quickly! I've no taste for another Alesia!" Sapinus replied, "We will cut them down in no time! "Caesar told him "Do not get too carried away. They are worth more alive than dead-as slaves. Those that do not surrender cut them off at the river and drown them like rats. Shackle the rest".

Sapinus saluted, shouted "Caesar!" and rode away. He called out to the Travari, to surrender." Men of Gaul. I ask you to surrender, and none will be killed and all treated with respect".

He waited, but none surrendered. They jeered back at him. Thereafter, Sapinus rode up and down behind his ranks, yelling orders. The thundering of seven thousand horses crashed into standing men front line of Treveri, throwing them under the horses' hooves, they're trampled to death as the next line of horses comes over them. Tullius then ordered his foot soldiers into the Treveri, effectively squeezing and boxing them in, pushing them back to the river. The Treveri were no pushover, they fight for singular honor but lacked cohesiveness as a fighting force. Eventually, they were pushed right into the river where many drowned. The survivors were rounded up, chained together, and whipped into submission, adding to the already-captured hundreds of thousands.

As the evening sun set, guards stood at the door, and servants brought in food and wine. All were warm, as fire burns on brazers inside the tents. The Generals met with Caesar and looked at maps of the area. Tullius, looked down at the map, said as he pointed, "We must winter here with the river to our backs. The wheat count is meagre. If we winter here, we can re-supply by sending slaves south and wheat north". Caesar, sitting and writing notes and replied without looking up "Good plan. We shall do as you recommend. however, in the meantime, shift to acorns for the slaves, buckwheat for the soldiers, and whatever fish we can get give to the men also. And take everything that you need from these Treverians. The more we enslave, the less debt I have to worry about". Always the clever wit, Anthony teasingly said

"You have defeated and laid waste to all of Europa and what do you do, but spend your time writing these love letters!" Caesar was irritated by this comment and stated, "Antony, you complain to a battle-weary old man. My pleasure is this woman. With her, the Egyptians and Egypt may be more stable. I aim to capture her heart. Consider it my bond with 'Alexander the Great'! Antony replied "And what is our big-nosed princess up to these days?"

Caesar replied,"Her flute-playing father has died. She is now a queen at eighteen and married to her brother, as the Ptolemies are want to do. This marriage is one marriage that I have to break soon. He is tied too closely with Pompey." Antony, picked up the scroll from Caesar's desk."But what have you written here?"

" Congratulations on your marriage to your brother. For your realm, try to concentrate on placating the population. May the Gods bless your reign with plentiful harvests".

Antony smiled and said well Cleopatra to send more wheat and beer'! He then handed the letter back to Caesar and added "Or we'll have problems this winter. Speaking of problems, we have nearly half a million slaves marching into Italia. It is time to lay the debts to rest and take Rome off my dear friends' hands".

11

46 BC. The Royal Barge passing the Pyramids

The Royal Barge set sail in a strong wind and headed further south. Cleopatra's pride in her country showed as she played the guide and in perfect Latin pointed out the Pyramids as they sailed by. "They were built far in the past, it is still wondered even now, how or why they were built," she said. They walked back to the cushions. Cleopatra lay down and popped grapes to Caesar's open mouth. Caesar propped himself up on one arm and looked at Cleopatra, "Cleo, do you consider yourself to be Greek or Egyptian?" Cleopatra considered the question carefully. "Well", she replied, "I was born here as were all my relatives over the last three hundred years. As a child I didn't live in Greece, but lived with Greek customs and people here. Alexandria's educated population is mostly new Greeks or old families that have been here since 'Alexandria the Great'. "My customs are a both Greek and Egyptian, but more importantly, I am the mother of all Egyptians and represent Isis the goddess that protects us all. Thus I am ...Egyptian!", she smiled. Caesar said nothing in return but reflected on the view and how lucky he finally was to see such wonders and travel the Nile, another great wish of his. "Now, I must leave you for a while, she whispered into his ear, my servants will shave me so that I may please you tonight", she laughed half in shyness and half teasingly. Caesar replied smiling" and I shall be your servant and wait" . Later, as the slave girls served them wine, he asked her "Just how did you leave the palace when you heard of your brother's plan". "Ah", she said, "that was the worst of times. As she thought back, she picked up a flower petal from the floor and one by one pulled out all the petals, and spoke.

49 BC. Fall-time, Alexandria, Egypt.

The Library in Alexandria is full of readers, some to study and some to flirt with others while pretending to study. There are now over seven hundred thousand manuscripts of all subjects. Here, Cleopatra loved to spend time reading medical documents for women ailments and poisons for her enemies. Suddenly as she studied, a pigeon arrived, back from its long flight from Europe. Apollodorus, now twenty-two, personal servant to Cleopatra, carried the returned pigeon to her. Apollodorus was an impressive figure, severe and lean. He took off the small rolled up letter from the pigeon's leg and went to hand it to Cleopatra, but it was snatched from his hand by Diogenes, her Greek adviser. Cleopatra looked at him with a quizzical smile and asked, "What does Caesar have to say?" Diogenes, at fifty-five years old, looked at the small letter and said, "He wishes you well and has conquered the far corners of the barbarian lands. He also wants you to call him... 'Uncle'"! Jahi, now aged forty-five, an Egyptian tutor with a military bearing, sat nearby, commented, "Take care with this Roman's familiarities."

Behind Cleopatra, sat her 'maids-in-waiting'. Charmion, a white girl from Cyprus at twenty-two years of age, who always smiled and next to her, Iris, a black Nubian girl, at twenty-one, rolled her eyes at this comment. Both were more than servants to Cleopatra, they were loyal friends and confidants. Cleopatra smiled, 'Uncle Caesar?' How nice. And I will take care. Well, now I would rather rest. Charmion, prepare my afternoon bath and Iris, I shall wear the new yellow dress tonight for my 20th birthday! Let's be all be happy!"

The following day in the Royal Hall Cleopatra sat on her throne with an empty throne beside her. Her staff and advisers next to her. Diogenes read her a letter from Caesar. Before her, citizens knelt on the floor, waiting patiently, to plead their cases. Cleopatra asked, "Diogenes, what has the dear 'Uncle Caesar written this time?'" Diogenes read the new letter,

"Basically, he demands that more beer and wheat be sent right away". Cleopatra looked at him, "I have just been made a queen, and he demands? Well, it is bad timing for this demand what with low Nile waters and no rain." Diogenes smiled, "What is the old saying...

'People don't eat jewels, they eat the bread made from the wheat that grows on the banks of the River Nile.'

Then for the first time that day, she looked up at a citizen and asked, "So what demands do you make, citizen?" The citizen was silent, the whole room on edge, waiting for him to speak. Cleopatra, firmly, but not unkindly stated, "As I understand it, you are petitioning to be exempted from the sacred tax, as your crops have failed? "

13

The citizen bowed and replied, "Yes, Your Majesty" Cleopatra looked at the man, she realized that her answer might mean the end of her hold on power if she did not give them the right reply. "You are exempted from all taxes'." There was an exclamation of shock from the whole room. Diogenes gasped "Majesty, the taxes are mandatory, for all the people!" Cleopatra turned to him "Do not question me. I am my people, and when they suffer, I suffer. Do you wish me to suffer?" Diogenes bowed deeply and said, "No, Majesty, may the great divinity forgive me". Cleopatra looked about at the crowd and stated "Let it be known that from this day forth all taxes are to be revoked for growers of grain and farmers of cows until we are again blessed with rains sufficient to flood our life-giving country. Let it be done"!

The room erupted in the cheers of citizens, the admonished advisers shared looks. She turned to an adviser, quietly "That concludes this day's affairs, bring me the paperwork later". Agitated, she got up to leave. All of the citizens immediately fell prostrate to the floor, her advisers bowed deeply. She looked to either side and walked majestically out of the room, followed by her people.

Cleopatra and her entourage walked down the hall, towards the Royal bedroom and bath. From around the corner appeared Ptolemy, her brother husband, now ten years old and aware of his power in a childish way. Beside him, his two advisers Polthinius, adviser on political matters, fifty years of age, garbed along with Achilles, forty eight, the boy's military adviser. They moved forward to confront Cleopatra. Pothinius stopped in front of her. "Majesty, we beg but a moment of your time." Cleopatra looked at him with a mixture of disgust and apprehension "I've no time to talk". Then, looking straight ahead, "The people's court is over.

I have dealt with enough trivial business for one day. I doubt anything you have to contribute will elevate my mood". Pothinuius replied "It is not a matter of court that we come to you for, as the divine one herself must know. We speak on behalf of your Co-regent, His Excellency the King, the Pharaoh, Ptolemy Theos Philopater, he of Sedge and Bee, he of...". Cleopatra, rolled her eyes". Oh, spare me!"

Cleopatra and her group come to a halt. She finally looks directly at Pothinius, then past him to her brother-husband, Ptolemy and smiles. Cleopatra looked at her brother, like a cat to a mouse. "Let me guess. My little husband doesn't like the newly devalued coins?" Achilles pipped in, "Ah, yes, the coinage which great Cleopatra saw fit to produce without his...ahem, consent. His Majesty has not yet had sight of it." Ptolemy standing behind his advisers, suddenly stated "Coins? What do you mean, coins? Achilles, what is my sister talking about?" Achilles turned to face the boy king." It... ah, seems there are new talents in circulation which bear only the image of the Queen, your Majesty. There must have been some mistake, which she will be sure to explain".

Ptolemy, about to pull a tantrum stuttered "I'm... not on...the...coins?" Cleopatra looked at him and said dismissively. "What was I to do, dear husband? You refuse to be in the same room as I, how were we to get an image of you? I didn't have any choice. I only did what I thought was best, sweet brother". Ptolemy pulled at Achilles' sword but was stopped. Even at ten, he understood what she was up to and replied "You go too far sister! I am not a child. I am a god! I am the true ruler of the greatest land in the world! You are merely my consort, and consorts can be replaced. That was the will of our father, as you well know and his will is the divine law"!

Pothinius turned to Ptolemy, trying to control the child. "Majesty, remember what we spoke of earlier? Let us return to your chambers and discuss this further, alone. Cleopatra, interrupting Pothinius angrily stated, "Consort, am I? So, where were you in court just now? Which one of us signs the decrees, rules the land, sets the taxes, listens to the people and their plight? And which one of us plays at king all day, hitting his minions with wooden swords while they whisper in his ear their pathetic schemes to further their ends? Enough. Clear this hall, I would leave this place... and you."

She moved to do just that. Cleopatra's guards move forward ahead of her. Ptolemy, angry but scared, turned and stomped away, followed by Pothinius. Achilles, however, remained and stood his ground, looking at Cleopatra. Achilles looked at Cleopatra. "Queen Cleopatra. I would advise against angering your king with 'your... games". Cleopatra turned to say something, but Achilles continued "May I remind you of the terms of your father, King Ptolemy's will? The decree was that to rule, his son must take you as his consort. Not the opposite. By my count, that makes you, how shall we say...surplus to requirements?" Achilles bowed deeply, gloating, while Cleopatra stood dumbstruck. She was visibly agitated by what he has just said, wanting to reply but unable. He turned and walked away with confidence reserved for those behind the throne.

46 BC. The Royal Barge near Herakleopolis.

The Royal vessels glided gracefully down the Nile, past the city of Herakleopolis and Theban Necropolis.

Caesar asked "who lies within there? "Cleopatra looked over at the buildings as they glided by and said "The graves of those highest and loyal the crown. Clerks, priests, overseers, priests, mayors' and prophets and many more. Their resting place has the honor of being close to the Nile so that even in their afterlife, they can see the mother waters". Caesar called for a towel to wipe his hands then asked, "And how about your family, where do they lie?" Cleopatra carefully folded his towel and put it aside. "My family lies near Alexandria. We built a walled temple, facing Greece, called 'Taposiris Magna', in honor of Osiris and Isis. I shall be buried here also when my time comes. But let us not dwell on this." Cleopatra, lay next to Caesar, stroked his thinning hair and asked "And what about you and of this Europa, your letters spoke of the great losses and gains you made there. Was there no gold or great monuments to their afterlives?" Caesar replied, "No gold could be found, certainly no monuments. These are simple barbarians but ah, they could put up a good fight. But my greatest triumphs came with great losses of friends. We sacrificed many men, fighting the Belgae, Germanians, and Gauls. Cleopatra pondered his reply, as her military lessons coming to mind, she replied laughing, showing her dimples, "When you crossed the Rubicon River with your scant leftover army, truly I thought you had gone too far, and I was about to lose my letter-writing 'Uncle'!".

Caesar looked at her, put his wine goblet down and replied, "Ah! That was my finest hour. I know Pompey well. He 'over-thinks', and while he did so, I moved quickly and seized the day, while he slept the night! I decided my fate...appealed to the God Jupiter and my men then advanced on Rome." His thoughts faded back to that fateful day and decision."

49 BC. Winter, Italy, Rubicon River.

The Rubicon River is found in the northeast of Italy and is a border of sorts. It ran full with spring waters, and as Caesar watched his vast army cross this river, Antony noted wryly, "We've truly made history today, for better or worse! The moment we crossed that river we became invaders and criminals! You know the rules, 'no army with arms, shall cross the Rubicon'. Caesar quietly replied, "We are criminals, only if we lose, friend. Only if we lose. Anyway, our army has crossed over so the 'die is cast!"

Tullius cantered up to join them. "Caesar, there are loyal Pompey troops atop the hill!" Antony looked at Caesar 'and said, 'He's onto us!' Sapinus jumped into the conversation, "I know Pompey. He has left here only older men and young boys. We can easily rout them". Caesar gave the orders to the cavalry. "Order them to kill only if they do not surrender, understand? Chase those boys off and send the scouts to Rome to see what they can find". Tullius looked at Caesar and stated before riding off, "Roman fighting Roman. May the Gods forgive us."

The hilltop battle lasts only a few minutes. Caesar's men rode uphill into the midst of Pompey's old men and boys, hitting instead of stabbing, causing quick panic and flight within Pompey's few troops. Caesar, Anthony, and the generals surveyed the fighting on the hilltop. Battle continued, both sides killing the wrong men, as the same uniforms confused all, as to who is who. Anthony rode back to Caesar and shouting out "What a bloody mess! And what about the slaves? There are far too many to trudge into Rome?!" To which Caesar replied "Keep the slaves near the river, sort out the 'wheat from the chaff'. Keep the best of the lot, especially the women for our 'dear banker friends'. The rest, hand out to the men".

Later that month. Caesar started to cough into a cloth as he wrote. A slave knelt by his side. Sapinus looked carefully at me him "You look sickly, Caesar. The camp is secured. Take a rest. No?" Caesar replied "I shall rest in Rome, now I need to think of the future. It may be within our grasp to take control of this empire...and that means Egypt too. Leave, and let me write." Antony chipped in from where he lay on the couch, playing with a young female servant. "He's never so sick that he can't write to her. Let me check your spelling". He rolled off the couch and walked over to Caesar's desk and took his letter and as he did, commented" Women have sharp minds, and she may see through you". He read Caesar's letter.

"Dear Cleopatra: By the time you get this letter, I will be either dead or the new emperor of Rome. I have crossed the Rubicon River and you know what that means. Now we camp in Roman territory with my army for the winter months. I must complete in Rome, what I have started. If I remain alive, I will send good tidings to you. Be careful what you do, for war is upon us all."

He handed the letter back to Caesar, pointing to one word," You have to correct that, and yes... she had better be careful". Caesar turned to the slave messenger, "Send this message to Cleopatra". "Yes, master, at once!" he replied. Antony, looked at Caesar "You're spoiling this child". "Maybe", Caesar said, "But when I replace Pompey, Egypt will be in my hands to place whomever I want on the throne and it may well be her".

49 BC. Alexandrian Palace.

In the Palace, Jahi pulled out a new message from Caesar, and read aloud to Cleopatra as they walk down the hallway, flanked by her people. She had her gaze fixed ahead of her as they walked. Cleopatra smiled and asked, "What does my 'Dear Uncle' have to say, and where is he?" Jahi replied, "He's entered Rome with his troops and bids you 'take care'. He will send word if he survives to fight Pompey in Greece". Cleopatra laughed" He asks me to take care!" Everyone laughed along with her as they entered her Royal Chambers. The night had come, a full moon rose outside and a small breeze from the ocean, cooled the daytime heat, making inside more pleasurable to be in.

The large suite of rooms contained tables, ornate furniture, statues of Greek figures both small and life-size and a grand bed. The guards remained outside the chambers. Cleopatra immediately started pacing about, very agitated, pulling at her headdress and jewelry to get them off. "Heavy is the head that wears the crown" my father used to say, she mumbled to herself. Exasperated, she called to her maids, "Help me!" Iras moved to her quickly 'A thousand apologies, "My lady" and helped her take off the heavy jewelry. Cleopatra continued to complain "It's coming, I know it's coming". Diogenes asked "Your Majesty?" To which Cleopatra replied as she paced about speaking quickly "The end of this farce of co-rulership! My soft-headed father must have known it would never work!"

How can I be free of this situation now, when the gods have done everything to thwart any expectations of prosperity? I have nothing left with which to appease our people". Diogenes did his best to keep pace with her, as she walked around in circles, he said "Oh Queen, had, the crops been bounteous these last summers, the people would see your reign as favorable. But it is you they blame for their misfortune. Whether you are goddess or mortal, they see you as the cause of drought and misery, and think your young brother should be allowed his turn to offer them salvation".

Cleopatra ceased her pacing, and turned to him in anger and said ".This is what you think, too? You think I am to blame for all of this? Because that is what it sounds like to me". Diogenes, backing up a bit replied, "Craving your pardon, Majesty, but no. I merely echo the voice of you're starving people. It need not be said that Achilles and Pothinius have had a hand in influencing the direction of your people's anger. 'And... then' there are the aid and troops you gave Pompey, a cause which is perceived to be against Egypt's own interests". Cleopatra looked at him and carefully, "I am divine, daughter of Ra, a descendant of Alexander himself. All I wish is to bring back the years of magnificence and prosperity of old. Don't you think I feel the weight of the Pharaohs on me? The Sphinx herself is judging me with her stare". Now, exasperated, she said" What am I supposed to do? My pubescent brother is dragging me down to his base level with his

19

pathetic, treacherous mewling. Did Ramesses have to contend with this? Nefertiti?" Jahi, jumped into rescue Diogenes, "Majesty, if I may say so, all you say is the truth. But, at this juncture, I fear it may be necessary to postpone the...expectation of future greatness, while we consider your immediate safety".

Cleopatra entered a large spacious bathroom, and stripped down, behind a thin curtain as her maids prepared her bath. She spoke to the other side of the curtain, where the men stand, averting their eyes. Cleopatra's voice started to raise with her temper, "What are you talking about, my safety? Look where we are! In my palace, surrounded by my guards, in my city. How could I not be safe?" Jahi again jumped in, "Again, begging leave, O Queen, the palace you share with your brother-husband, sharing his guards, his city. At this moment, it seems his word holds greater sway." Cleopatra entered her bath but kept talking from behind the curtain as the maids applied soap to her. "Greater sway? Who is the one who sits in the throne while he flicks dead flies at his tutors all day long? I! I am queen, he is a plaything of his puppet masters".

Jahi replied carefully over the curtain, "Not so, O Queen. His advisers have been gathering support at court and, as you know, the head of your army is Achilles. His right-hand man". Furious, Cleopatra rose from her bath "Are you trying to tell me he is going to depose me? Kill me? If anyone around here is going to dispose of their sibling, it is going to be I. I just hadn't planned on it so soon!".

Jahi gestured for Diogenes to do the talking, unseen by Cleopatra behind the curtain. Both were sweating from both steam heat and fear of her temper. Jahi carefully replied "I would not consider that advisable in this particular instant, great Queen. The people would surely object". Finally, Diogenes spoke-"I believe the people's wrath is not helped by their belief that you are a pawn of Rome". Cleopatra slid back into the pool with her maids resuming washing her and replied", I know that. How dare you think I do not? Surely I could never be so despised by my people that they would harm me? They love me, as I love them! Tiny, mortal insects they may be, but they are my insects. I shall shelter them in my hive as long as I draw breath. They would never rise up against me"!

Diogenes replied carefully, "Undoubtedly, Majesty. But yet I think it unwise to tempt them, or the gods, by such a bold move. My informers tell me that your brother's people have planted dissenters amongst the city, readied the army and are plotting to arrest you on the morrow". The face of Cleopatra showed the sudden devastation. "How could I not have been informed of this sooner?" she said. Jahi moved forward and talked over the curtains, "We have only recently garnered intelligence of this. Until we were sure of the severity of the situation, we did not want to trouble you unnecessarily, over the stresses of state until we were sure what was to transpire". Cleopatra existed her bath, and donned with the help of her maids put on her night clothes, then came around the

20

curtain to face her advisers. Cleopatra regained her composer and said rather sarcastically "I see, so...what do you suggest, then?" Diogenes and Jahi look at each other, then Diogenes nodded and replied "To leave, Majesty".

Cleopatra, shocked at his reply, shouted, "Leave! Leave Alexandria?" The advisers remained silent, bowed their heads slightly. Other attendants look shocked. But Cleopatra looks merely baffled, then amused. "Just like that? One day I'm conducting affairs of state, and the next I'm on a camel, a boat, or lying around in a villa in Cyprus, perhaps?

Leaving my country and for how long? Where to? To do what? Oh, and how about another question, when?" Jahi answered her 'tonight'. She laughed hysterically, starting to pace again, water dripping from her hair. "Tonight? Why of course! I'll just have my things packed, and we'll be off. An imperial palace doesn't take long to pack, after all. Make sure to bring only the second best formal place settings, the gold ones are ever so heavy!" Diogenes, nervous, started to fidget'. "We are not suggesting a movement of the whole palace, Majesty".

Cleopatra eyed Diogenes, "We? Since when do we not include me, pray to tell? Who is your queen and what has been going on behind my back, amongst my most trusted advisers?" Jahi, spoke quickly, "You alone are our Queen, Majesty. It is for precisely this reason that our informants have kept a constant vigil on Ptolemy's inner circle. If you do not leave of your own accord now, he will expel or kill you with the people's support behind him." Diogenes butted in, "Therefore, we believe, for your sacred place in the lineage of your ancestors, that you must leave of your own volition. So that you may appeal to your father's loyal friends and neighbors to support your rightful claim to Egypt's throne and we must also take Arsinoe, as she may replace you on the throne if left here. We can keep her under guard in Pelusium until you decide what to do with her. Killing her is not advised, she is too popular. Jahi, "We have sent envoys to the Roman Governor in Syria to expect your arrival. Though, given the conflict between Caesar and Pompey, we are unsure of their ability to receive you". Cleopatra moved over to a table and chair, where she sat down slowly, and let her face sink into her hands. Her 'ladies in waiting' come to her side kneeled at her feet. Cleopatra, looked at Diogenes, "I see, yes, my sister. I cannot dispose of yet, but as you say, we must take her by trickery. We can keep her locked up at Pelusium in Gaza until I return I suppose. Some extract of poppy will keep her quite." She Looked up at the sky" The clouds are parting. Against my own heart, my instincts. I begin to see now that what you say makes sense. May the gods... forgive my pride. Her face sank once more into her hands, her words barely audible. "How can it be that I am to leave Alexandria? I cannot imagine even existing for one moment outside of its walls. Since I became queen, this has been my life, even more than before I took the throne". Diogenes approached her "So shall it be again, Majesty. When you have returned, we will have a fortune on our side. It shall not be many moons before you return"

Cleopatra replied, "Is this why some of the Royal Guard was moved to Pelusium recently? Were you preparing this? To steal away to Syria like my father before me?"

Jahi, smiled" Yes, O Queen. There was some need for preemptive preparation, enough to make a smooth passage for you, but not sufficient to arouse your husband's suspicions. Cleopatra tried to think "I suppose I should thank you in some way. There will be time enough for that later, I suppose. As for leaving, just how I am to depart this city? Do you plan on seeing your divine queen disguised as a servant girl perhaps, or a slave? Because you can forget that right away. I am a queen, and I will leave my city as a queen." Diogenes, "Great Cleopatra, the boy king has his servants everywhere. I do not think it wise to let it be known that you are leaving the palace. He will see it as a chance to attack you. "Cleopatra laughed for once" Which is not without its irony, considering the circumstances".

Jahi replied, "Yes, Mistress. To have been betrayed by your brother-husband, who deigns to opportunistically seize power when the tides turn against you. Nothing will perplex or vex him more than your mysterious absence tomorrow, preventing him from carrying out his plans for you." Cleopatra replied, "So, if not as a servant girl, what then? I am not to crawl on my hands and knees all the way out, am I?" Apollodorus, her male servant, stepped forward and stood at attention.

Diogenes said, "Your loyal servant Apollodorus has a suggestion, Mistress, which you may find suitable. Cleopatra 'What is it, Apollodorus? Speak!" Apollodorus licked his lips in nervousness "Divine Queen, I am a frequent sight around the palace, carrying things of great size or weight. No guard or servant pays me any heed" Cleopatra, looked carefully at him, "I don't see where this is going. You may be invisible, but I am rather the opposite."

Apollodorus, now even more nervous replied "Apologies, your Majesty. My meaning is, this one's invisibility may be our advantage. If I were to... secretly carry you and your drugged sister out of the palace, we would all be completely unnoticed. "Cleopatra thought carefully. "Secret? As in, hidden? Covered up in something?" No one answered, and she starts to walk and pace, apparently thinking it over. The others look to each other nervously, waiting for her to carry on. Cleopatra looked kindly upon Apollodorus and replied, "You no doubt feared my anger, Apollodorus. You need not fear, I understand at last what it is I have to do to save myself. I shall still be Queen wherever I go!". There was an audible sigh of relief.

Both Diogenes and Jahi instantly said, "May it be always so, Majesty. "Cleopatra looked at everyone in the room "So, it is settled. Except for one thing. Not tonight, but early tomorrow morning. I will have one more night in my palace. Make the arrangements."

She waved her hand to dismiss them and turned away. Jahi mumbled "All praise to you, great Queen. "The advisers and Apollodorus bowed and left, leaving only with Cleopatra and her 'ladies in waiting'.

Cleopatra entered her bedchambers in her nightgown. Her 'ladies in waiting', tidying, laying out her night clothes, fussing over her. Cleopatra looked at them and said, "Leave it. Tonight of all nights, you do not have to tidy this room. We will all be gone by morning, gods save us. That little wretch of a brother can concern themselves with this mess. I almost want to trash it, to deny him the pleasure of rifling through my things".

Iras smiled "Yes, Cleo. I have prepared your traveling wardrobe the best I can, though I don't know...will you need this?" Iras, Cleopatra's chief hairdressing girl, held up a cobra headdress. Cleopatra smiled and shook her head. "I doubt it, somehow. I do not see myself wearing that on camel's back in the desert". Iras smiled and said, "No, my lady. How silly of me, forgive me. May I dry and brush your hair now?" Cleopatra, now looking tired, said, "Yes, you may. Only the gods know the next time I will sit in front of a golden mirror, having my hair brushed. It is going to be hard, going from being the queen of Egypt to... whatever I will be out there." Cleopatra sat down on an ornate chair, closed her eyes. Iras came to stand behind her, began and slowly brushed Cleopatra's hair. Cleopatra, looked pale, "I feel sick to my stomach at the thought this is my last night here until gods know when. I never thought I would be leaving like this. I had lived here my whole life, except for when I was very young in Rome".

Iras gently replied, "In Rome?" Cleopatra stopped talking, got up and moved over to the bed. The ladies-in-waiting put out the torches and came and lie down with her. "Tomorrow I leave Alexandria and must be born again. As a rebel queen, a savior of her people. I must hide, fight, win friends and rally armies. Gods know what else. So just this one last night, I would be soothed as a child by her mother. Who among you can do that?"

Charmion offered. "If I may have the honor. I know a story about Queen Nefertiti, mother to Pharaohs and most beloved by all her people, and the mother cobra she met in the olive grove." "Cleopatra's eyes stared up at the ceiling, "Yes, tell me that one. I remember my mother telling it to me, long ago now. I've forgotten most of it since". Then closing her eyes, "How did she know the snake was a mother?" Charmion replied "Because Nefertiti was Isis, the great mother herself, and she possessed the gift of perceiving a mother's love in all living things. In the grove, she asked the Cobra where her children were...". Cleopatra slowly drifted off to a restless sleep.

23

46 BC. The Royal Barge near Thebes.

The Royal barge floated down the centre of the Nile River, the sun, now low in the West. Cleopatra and Caesar sat and sniffed lotus flowers that she had introduced to him. It helped relax him and prepare him for bedding later on. A servant woke her from her stupor and pointed towards the bank on the west side. She got up and in an excited voice said: "We will stop here on the east side to take in food and I want to show you the 'Temple of Thebes' dedicated to fertility and make a personal prayer". They disembarked, and as they walked towards the temple, she took his arm and told him of the temple's history. "Here, my gentle Caesar, lay three thousand years of dead kings and queens". As they entered the temple, Caesar asked, "What is that smell?" Cleopatra took him by the hand and replied `Kyphi' it is used as a temple fragrance". "and what does the fragrance contain" he again asked?" Cleopatra sat down with him near the front of the temple and replied as she ticked off the ingredients on her fingers, "a touch of old wine, honey, myrrh, two grams of raisins, juniper berried, sweet flag, camel grass and four parts of aspalathos." Caesar laughed, "Someday you will make a fine guide. Can you name all the pharaohs?"

Cleopatra thought for a moment then replied, "No, no. There are so many buried here. It is not used today but was a thousand or more years ago. Only the names of visitors are easy to find on the walls. You can place your name next to so many others!" she joked. They both laughed. "And now I must pray for your son to come to my womb", and with that, she got up and disappeared with the white-robed, bald, priests.

By the time they had returned to the ship. The decks had been swept clean, and more rose flower petals were strewn here and there on the upper deck and in the pool below deck. Both were hot and sweaty. Cleopatra took Caesar by the hand led him below where naked female servants waited. Caesar and Cleopatra stripped-off with the help of the servants. Cleopatra stepped naked in a pool of asses milk. She laughed at the expression on Caesar's face upon seeing the pool of milk, as she explained how good it was for the skin. The servant's women, giggled to see his expression and urged him to get in with more giggles and soft hands, guided him into the pool. He smiled in embarrassment, not being accustomed to being naked with his love and a trove of naked servant girls, barely out of their teens.

He swam over next to Cleopatra and needing time to relax his loins, turned his back to her. She picked up a blue glass small vase and proceeded to wash his hair. "What are you washing my hair with!", he asked?

She replied "it's a mix of calves blood, horn of gazelle, backbone of a raven, boiled in oil. Soon your hair will soon grow back" .Later she rubbed oil onto his face. "And that is ?" he asked, between pats to his face. "It's Lupin seed oil and will rejuvenate your face skin my handsome husband, she laughed.

Caesar closed his eyes and replied, smiling, "Woman, you will spoil me!" She smiled widely then left him and moved to the edge of the bath and sat on the side, and asked in a more serious tone, "What happened to you and your army before you arrived into Rome?" He replied, "I came close to meeting the same fate of being buried, like the kings here, had I not taken on Pompey and defeated him". His gaze turned inward as he thought about those tumulus times in Rome, on the march and the outcome.

49 BC. Winter to Spring, Rome.

In mid-winter, after weeks of marching, Caesar's army entered Rome and found a ghostlike city with fearful residents hiding behind closed doors. Sapinus rode up beside him and commented quietly "Seems the plebs are apprehensive. They know not what we are up to". They passed an armory with scattered weapons left unattended.

The doors to the Senate lie ajar, papers littered the stairs of the abandoned building. Antony moved his horse close to Caesar and with his usual wit, said sarcastically "And where be mighty Pompey and his army?" Caesar commented "He's fled to Greece, I'm sure of it, and now this has created confusion for Rome's people, so we'd best be careful. I don't want an uprising". Then he turned to a nearby Scribe, "Post a dictum on the Senate doors and write, "There will be peace. None need fears retribution. The scribe bowed quickly "At once, Sire".

The austere Roman Senate chamber looked run-down, leaves lay outside and in,on unwashed floors. Here, a few senators remained, in unkept togas and Caesar with his entourage, discussed the matters at hand. Young Cicero, at sixty-one, the Speaker of the Senate, spoke in hushed tones to those few presents. "We starve as we sit. Pompay, his army and government have all left eastward towards Greece. Mighty senators, we must repair this situation before we resort to eating the slaves that you, Caesar brought back with you! Let us vote to attack Pompay!" Tittering was heard from a few. Sitting off to the side Servius called out, "Like your great-uncle, you speak so eloquently.

However, it is not the Gauls we face, but instead the might of Rome, and Roman against Roman? Who knows the outcome? With us outnumbered three to one". Tulius, muttered from the side, "I say, leave them, let them drink Greek piss and rot. We hold the Senate and Italy. They have abandoned their roles here, we are now the legitimate rulers and you, Caesar, need to rest". Caesar sat perched on his consular chair made the decision to move forward before his army's swords, turned to rust. "No, my dear colleagues, no rest. We must now make haste and hope that Pompey's army has become complacent. He has more than double the men, but they lack fighting experience. Let us take the war to Pharsalos. Let us vote as Young Cicero suggested!"

Later that month, before they left for Greece, Caesar asked the generals for a count of weapons and food supplies. Antony, looked at the papers before him "We have three and one-half cohorts and one thousand eight hundred horses and horsemen, about twenty-two thousand men. Oh, and we have two new prefectus and two new tribuni. Also new centurians who come with little experience." Caesar then asked" And what about arms, Tulius?" Tulius replied, "We have plenty of helmets, shields, large swords, daggers, javelins, but we do lack short swords, bowmen, bearera, crossbows.

26

There has not been enough time to make or find more". Caesar then looked at Serius, "And food supplies?" Serius, read out the list. "We have, plenty of fish, flour, dates, honey, but we lack in bread and meat". Caesar looked at the lists and then looked up," This had better be a quick fight, or we will be in the embarrassing position of starving to death first. Let's get ready to march".

Caesar marched with his troops, through Illyria, on their way to fight. Late one night, he started convulsing, it was an epileptic fit. An ill omen should the soldiers find out. Tullius kept him in his tent and told a slave, "Get the physician, quickly, say nothing to anyone, on pain of death!" The slave quickly replied, "Yes, Sire!" and made haste. Later, that night, the fit having evidently subsided, the physician rose from the bed where from inspecting Caesar, stated, "Caesar has the affliction again. It's the stress". Antony turned to the Generals and even in Caesar's condition was able to joke "It's more like his Egyptian love, he worries she has changed her mind as women want to do". The physician ignored Antony and replied, "I have heard of the great Pyramid of Illyria, some say its older than the Egyptian ones and that the top contains healing energy, Let us take Caesar there before we lose him".

And so, they agreed and in the middle of the night took him up the mysterious mountain that supposedly gave the weak, life-giving forces.

The Generals carried Caesar first by carriage than on foot to the top of the grassy pyramid mountain, not using torches, in the pitch black night made it difficult and dangerous. Climbing around rocks and trees, they finally reached the top. The physician whispering all the way carry him up "Please be careful with him". Antony, bearing most of my weight said rather agitated" This had better work, or we will toss you off this pile of rock!" Servius called out suddenly, "We are at the top, bring up the Sear quickly". The Sear, explained to all, "Energy flows from within this pyramid mountain, lay him down and I will chant to the Gods". Antony replied. "Then let's do this, if the men find out, they will be heading home without us!" The Sear begins his prayers, and after an hour Caesar recovered slowly. Antony knelled beside him and asked" How do you feel?" Caesar weakly replied. "I dreamed that I met Alexander the Great and he has blessed me and my plans" and looking about added, "Let's get off this mountain, we have a war to win". With relief, they finally headed back to camp.

46 BC. The Royal Barge near Ramses the Third Temple.

Later on, the Nile, as they reached the halfway point, Cleopatra suddenly pointed to the coastline, "oh! Caesar! There is the 'Temple of Ramses the Third! 'He was just like your favorite Greek, 'Alexander the Great!'. He lived a thousand years ago and is considered the father of Egypt. See his statue, so grand and red, reflecting the sunlight!" "Very poetic", Caesar replied. "Oh!', Cleopatra, suddenly remembered." I have written a poem for you, in Latin, do you want to hear it?" "Please," replied Caesar. She read from the papyrus paper.

"My heart knows your love, while only half my temple is plaited. I hasten to know you, and my hairdo becomes undone. But I shall don a perfumed wig and will be ready at any moment, for you".

"Do you like it, she asked?" Caesar shaded his eyes, and looked at her, then reached over and kissed her said, "Your Latin is better than mine, and yes, I loved it!". Then he asked "But tell me, how did you escape the clutches of your brother?" Cleopatra, frowned, "That was a terrible week" .She looked down at her nails and reflected back.

49 BC. Fall Time, The Palace and Beyond.

The Palace corridor was dark, lit only by torches. Two palace guards faced each other on either side of the passage, holding spears. At the end of the corridor, Appolodorus and a trusted friend came into view, with a bundle over their shoulders. They strode with purpose, and as they got close to the guards, the guards looked at each other, then flickered their eyes towards Appolodorus, and back at each other. Appolodorus smiled at the guards and slowed his pace and said, "The Queen deigned to throw her wine goblet on the carpets, and now the sight of it offends her. Easy come easy go, eh". The guards smiled knowingly and made no move to stop them. Appolodorus smiled at them as he kept going, past them and down the corridors and around the corners and finally into a tunnel.

Appolodorus and his friend, held the bundles carefully as they keep moving but the tunnel was not wide, so occasionally one end or other brushed or bumped against the wall. Once or twice when it bumped, little squeaks or grunts came from out of the carpets, followed by a muttered apology from Appolodorus" begging your pardon, Majesty, craving your apology great Queen, Sorry! Sorry!"

Appolodorus and friend emerged from a small doorway in the palace wall, stopped, look left and right, then headed towards the small dock. As they approached the dock, where a boat waited for them, with oarsmen dressed humbly, who, when seeing the men, sat down and waited with oar ready. Cleopatra's maids and advisers also sat in the boat, dressed in simple clothes, waited and worried.

Appolodorus came to the water's edge and passed the carpets to the men in the boat. They lay them down gently in the ship, everyone looks at each other in trepidation. Iras whispered, "Aren't they going to get out of the carpets?" Diogenes whispered back "No, we stick to the original plan! There are still too many risks. What if we're seen on the river by a fisherman, a patrol, anyone! It's bad enough that we are traveling together, but at least there's a chance no-one will recognize us. Her majesties stay hidden until we leave the shore. They can get out in a few minutes". The oarsmen cast off, and started to row across the Nile River, into the rising sun as they silently as possible, and headed eastward to Gaza on the eastern side.

Everyone was silent, the ladies, fell asleep on each other. The rowers look tired, and Appolodorus and the advisers sat tensely. Partway over, there was a scuffle from the area of the carpets and muffled screaming and rustling. Appolodorus whispered 'We must get them out" and moved to open both carpets up "Majesty, calm yourself, you are safe! We will release you, please be calm". Jahi called out, "is it safe? How can you be sure?" Appolodorus, unravelled the carpet, looked panicked, "We are far away from anyone, and

29

it's too hot in these carpets for them!" The ladies-in-waiting woke up and helped with getting Cleopatra out of the carpet while Arsinoe lay quietly, still drugged and sleeping.

Cleopatra emerged with some panting and shoving, then sat up, looking somewhat the worse for wear, but with a regal expression. Her people move back from her, and all bowed as far down as possible, given the constraints of the boat. Appolodorus sat back to give her room, bowed and said, "O Queen, our plan was successful, we are clear of Alexandria and the threat of your brother. It is now but a little further until the safety of the other shore, where nobody but your loyal guard will be expecting you". Cleopatra said nothing, covered in sweat, she brushed her hair with her fingers and turned to the direction of Alexandria, and moved to the edge of the boat, and under her breath, tears in her eyes, she muttered "My Alexandria!, oh...my Alexandria" and stifled her tears that fell on her sad face.

Sunrise came to the eastern shore of the Nile. Gaza was quite, no fishermen fished, no crocodiles or frogs. The beachhead was bleak, dark sand and stones. The rowers fussed over the boat, tying it up and taking out the packs. Appolodorus took the packages further onto the beach. The ladies stood nearby, quietly. Everyone looks concerned. Appolodorus was looking particularly worried and kept looking at Cleopatra. Eventually, he stooped what he's was doing and said, "My Queen, we cannot delay. We must move as far east as we can, by sunset, before word spreads of your esca... departure... please... Majesty?" Cleopatra stood near the water's edge facing Egypt She looked steadfastly then turns to her advisers and ladies. Focused on a single point, jaw clenched, she said with determination in her voice, "All you with me now, loyal citizens of my court, sworn to my service and my reign, and all the gods above and below, bear witness to me, and hear me now". All in view got on the ground to bow but for Arsinoe, who was now tied up and sat half awake with a gag in her mouth, showing her feelings with eyes that could kill.

Cleopatra, held one fist high, spoke very slowly, "I shall return. And I swear, those who opposed me, threatened me, or sought to destroy me, will perish, each one of them!" Silence came from everyone still on the ground. Cleopatra lowers her fist and her head, almost bowed to Alexandria, almost sobbed but managed to contain it. Eventually, she lifted her head, and turned around, to the sight of her camel guard a short distance away. She walked towards them with her head held high, as if she is starting afresh. The leader of the Royal Guard, Ekmet, the eunuch, dismounted from his camel, approached her quickly and went into a deep kneeling bow and said quietly, "Queen Cleopatra, I am Ekmet. My soldiers, behind me, are few but are all sworn in fealty to you only. We are to be your escort to the lands of Syria".

Cleopatra turned to her advisers behind her, and they bowed, slightly in agreement, except Arsinoe who scowled silently. Cleopatra seemed to have gotten over the shock of running away. Sober, she spoke "Good, then let's make haste, take some men and deliver my sister to Pelusuim and guard her carefully and the rowers...send them to Isis with my plea for help". The Royal guards got off their camels and walked over to the rowers, who now sat on the beach.

They walked behind the rowers, drew their swords.The rowers understood the sacrifice they had to make and only looked at Cleopatra. She turned them, smiled, as a mother would to her children and said, "You have served me well. Isis will protect you, and I will protect your families". They gave up their necks. The rowers died to the man with a sword to their neck and quickly buried nearby. Ekmet walked with Cleopatra to her camel and helped her onto it. Everyone else mounted up as well. The main group start riding away. The rest of the camel guard held back and rode off to towards the coast, and Pelusuim fort where more loyal guards waited for Arsinoe, who's the last look at Cleopatra was a glare, a mixture of fear and hate.

Cleopatra and her small group, travelled from eastern Nile shores, for ten days, and starlit nights, into the Judean area towards a Roman garrison. At the end of the tenth day, they were tired, hot and dirty from their long fast journey. Ekmet led them all to an oasis to freshen up. Ekmet's camel moved next to Cleopatras'. "We can rest and freshen up here for a few hours. "He said. To which she replied, "Thank you Ekmet, you have done well."

The ladies undressed while some of the Royal Guards, young women in they're the early twenties, either stood guard or also disrobed to wash. The women enter the water naked, laughing while the maids helped wash Cleopatra, a bit further away. Suddenly, there was a commotion. A small group of bandits enter the oasis by foot. Hand to hand combat ensued between the five bandits and the half naked Royal Guard. The bandits were shocked to find that the guards they were fighting, were all female. Grunts, cries, screams echo all about, with swords clashing against swords. Cleopatra and the maids try to hide in the reeds, their heads just above the water. Just as suddenly, a squad of Roman soldiers, appeared, and seen by the bandits, then fled with the Romans giving chase.

A few seconds later, a few more Romans entered into the Oasis water area and stopped to stare at the women. Their leader, General Bibulus, saw the naked women in the water with Cleopatra, who was now trying to get out of the water without exposing herself. Bibulus looked bemused "Welcome, 'Queen of Exile,' if I may call you that? "Jahi, standing nearby said quickly, "I must object!"

Cleopatra, while trying to cover herself up and looking a bit ridiculous, replied, "Whatever else? I am still Queen! But thank you for your timing!" Bibulus smiled, "Your welcome. Now please be my guest and get dressed, before the bandits reappear".

Later that day, in the Roman fort and Bibulus's office, they argued. Bibulus looked at the papers on his desk, "As you can see, we have concerns of our own what with the Caesar and Pompey's civil war". Cleopatra replied, "I understand your dilemma, do you understand mine?" .Bibulus looked carefully at her and replied, "In my defense, your brother is currently the King... Pharaoh in Alexandria, and you are in exile. Given Rome's current turmoil's, there is little reason for us to involve our self's in sibling rivalry at the present moment".

Cleopatra, paused, changed tack, "Siblings we might be, but it is Egypt's fate which hangs in the balance, and my fate is in your hands. I require your help along with your army!" Bibulus quickly stated, "And it is in the name of the current Senate, that I am to neither do you harm, nor hold you against your will or to help you with my forces, sorry. Of course by the laws of hospitality, you and your people are welcome to rest here, as long as you wish".

Cleopatra screwed up her mouth, "We came for an army, and you offer us cushions and cakes!" Bibulus gritted his teeth, trying to remain patient, replied "I cannot promise anything, as we are shortly to join Caesar in pursuing the remains of Pompey's forces. Our position here is in a state of flux, but as long as we are here, you are welcome. Also, I would be grateful for your answer soon as I really do have a lot to do". Cleopatra remained composed."Very well, I see I will get nowhere with you. It seems I should be standing in front of Caesar right now if I actually want anything beyond platitudes. This is not my first experience of Roman hospitality, and it seems to have changed in a few short years. You may show me to my rooms now". Bibulus fussed with his papers as he didn't expect to take her there himself. Stepping away from the desk, he moved towards Cleopatra. Her people step forward, alarmed but she turns and shoo'd them away saying "Go and see to my things. I would walk with the general alone". They then walked together through an open corridor.

Bibulus tried to calm the situation by talking about her father. "We received your father here not so long ago. I thought him an admirable..." Cleopatra jumped in, 'flute player?" Bibulus chuckled "I was going to say, 'man'. You do seem to have more of a king about you than Ptolemy, if I may speak plainly". Cleopatra returned the smile and said, "You may". Bibulus went on "Your sister Berenice married my friend General Archelaus while your father was here".

Cleopatra grimaced "I don't think it was a particularly long-lived marriage". Bibulus went on" Indeed. It was soon afterwards your father returned with our forces to attack them, led by myself and Mark Antony. Killing them was a messy business, unfortunate I thought." Cleopatra thought a bit then said "Mark Antony yes, I remember him. I thought him a brute. But my older sister deserved to die. She had betrayed my father. As my brother has betrayed me". Bibulus remained diplomatic and said, "Your family is not without its problems, I see".

To which she replied quickly, "We are all raised to be kings and queens, and therefore have no option but to fight for our place in history. Your system does not follow lines of ancestry as ours does... we are descended from the gods. In Rome, it seems, even a fishmonger may become a senator. I don't see your country lasting long".

Bibulus laughed and said" Time will be the judge of that, Queen Cleopatra. This is where I will leave you. I will do my utmost to see that you are provided for, by way of recompense. Please consider Lake El Talqah your home for now". They arrive at Cleopatra's quarters. At the doorway, Cleopatra turned and smiled, "It is hardly what I travelled all this way for, but I appreciate your gesture. Later on, you must tell me more about Caesar, he intrigues me. You may leave me now." Bibulus took the order in stride and swallowed his pride saying, "Majesty, please make yourself comfortable. If you need anything, ask for me personally". He left her looking discontented and frowning.

The next night, as the moon rose in the night sky, the courtyard became busy with men and her guards, loading up the camels with provisions and water. Cleopatra, now refreshed, clean and fed, turned to her people to see if they were all mounted, packed and ready to go. They were. Bibulus and a few other Romans stood nearby prepared to see them off. Bibulus approached Cleopatra and looked up at her"I am sorry you could not stay longer, Queen Cleopatra. She looked down at him and replied, "Comfortable as it is here if I cannot persuade you to join my cause, and I can see that I can't, then I cannot tarry here while my brother and Achilles gather strength in Egypt".

Bibulus, shook his head"I do understand, and can only apologize for our lack of resources. If it were my decision, I would much rather stop fighting my fellow Romans and take up arms against your brother. He sounds like a piece of work".

Cleopatra, smiled, and in jest, replied "You're not wrong. Though of course, I should have you killed for insulting the royal family. I will turn a blind eye, however, just this once." Smiling and bowing Bibulus replied, "Thank you, your Majesty". Cleopatra whipped the side of her camel and rode out of the courtyard, with Bibulus and his men looking on. Bibulus looked at his right-hand man and said, "I'm almost sorry to see her go. No women here for months, and then the next one to come through is the queen of Egypt, no less! I look forward to seeing what Caesar makes of her". The men smile at each other and turn back towards the building.

33

Cleopatra wore a desert-style scarf around her head and neck, a long kaftan, with pearls around her neck, with her followers behind her, all dressed in desert garb.

They made a train 30-or-so deep and travelled quickly, as they had over four hundred kilometers by camel to get to Lake Al Talqah in the northeast and along the way before meeting with local desert leaders. Beneath billion cold stars and broad Milky Way, lighting the way, they fled into the nights. The moon at times, large in the night sky, laid the way for them but other times, Ekmet had to use the stars to guide them.

Stopping here and there, they lay next to their warm camel's body, eating only dried raisins and dried apricots, she gazed above at the wonders of the night sky, the shooting stars and so deep into space where only the Gods resided and wondered how beautiful if we could all just fly like the birds. Apollodorus pulled his camel up to pull abreast of Cleopatra and asked "Do you care to rest, my Queen? We could take shelter. I fear for your comfort since leaving the Roman compound", Cleopatra smiled, "No, we must reach King Azar`s camp, or risk him moving again. After our disappointment with the Romans, I need this. I need him. Once he is behind us, the rest of the tribes will follow".

Apollodorus bowed his head and said smiling, "you wish Majesty. You need but speak, and your command will be fulfilled". Cleopatra smiled warmly at her favorite male servant and still looking straight ahead replied, "You know, we're not in Alexandria anymore, Appolodorus. Look at us, look at me. I am not cradling the sceptre on my lap, and I doubt very much if Isis ever looked like I do now". He replied, "Your Majesty? I do not comprehend?" Cleopatra looked at his from her camel saddle and complained

"You males are all alike" but kindly added "Of course you don't. How could you? You have known nothing but service, haven't you. What I mean is, it's hot, dry and as dull as anything I've ever seen. I have no entertainers, tumblers, dwarfs, Nubian or otherwise to amuse me on these long days of riding, camping. Maybe, just this once, amuse me. Tell me about yourself. Appodorus looked rather shy and looked behind him to see if anyone was listening replied, "I am not sure what it is I could amuse you with." Cleopatra rolled her eyes. For goodness sake, just talk! I'm not asking you to sing or dance, just say something. My mouth is dry, and I do not care to talk any further"!

Appolodorus meekly said, "Very well, my lady", He paused to think for a moment then said, "You speak the truth about my service. In far times, I was not a slave. My father was a mosaic artist in Elis and my mother a teacher of the flute. I was born in Athens. I went to school and learned Latin, read the stories of Homer and also studied the flute from my mother. But we ran into hard times. The area we lived in was raised to the ground to make way for an Olympic venue. With seven children to feed, my father sold me off to a Greek merchant, who kept me for four years and then when I was ten years of age, he sold me to your Royal Household, where I became one of your servants".

34

Cleopatra took a swig of water and some dates to eat and extended some to Appolodorus , as he took some she asked: "What did you eat in Athens as a child?" Appolodorus thought for a moment. It was a long time ago, but I remember my favorite food was dates with honey for dessert, sometimes we had pasteli, Medjools, and bread. On some occasions, usually the day of rest, we ate teganites with walnuts and honey. My father usually drank cheap wine while we children had goats milk. When I became a slave, my food changed to fish and more fish. To be truthful, I never want to see a fish again!

We never had much meat when I was a child, but there was plenty of honey. Now, all I eat is goat meat, maybe I will change to fish when we get back, he laughed"! On the tenth star-studded night of travel, dawn broke over the desert, soon the blazing hot sun would rise, making it too hot to ride. Usually, they would rest and wait for the late afternoon before starting out again, but as they ride onward towards Lake el Talqah, Jahi suddenly called out " Over there! I see a glint on the horizon." Cleopatra opened the curtain on her camel box and looked out, "Finally, we have may have Azar in our sight. Just a few more minutes closer and we will tell if it's another one of your hallucinations, Jahi, or not" she called back to him.

Then, turning to Appolodorus, she said: "I have to tell you, Appolodorus, our first encounters with these desert so-called-leaders have not inspired me in the least, especially the last Sheik!", she shuddered, and Appolodorus replied "He of the Western Hills, Majesty?" Cleopatra pulled a face "Yes, a real hill troll. He virtually laughed me out of his camp. I offered him a place in my court if he assisted me. Think of it, he and his camels, goats, and an army of ruffians, tramping through Alexandria. I'm almost glad he refused me in the end.

I can't believe what I am being forced to associate with... Is this what I have come to?" Jahi rode closer and comes to speak conspiratorially with Cleopatra. Jahi shouted to her" Majesty! If this is indeed King Azar, should we discuss the finer details of negotiations?" She called back" There are not many things, I would not grant him to gain his favor, and they are not up for discussion."

Jahi pressed on" I merely wished to go over the finer details, for example, do you plan on granting him dominion over any part of your lands. Cleopatra snapped back "Let's just see how amenable he is, to begin with, shall we? Then we can see what side his bread is buttered on. She then smiled, looked ahead, and spurred on her camel onward.

Finally, they arrived at King Azar's camp. King Azar, as he was referred to, out of respect for his authority over desert tribes, more than his power and riches, was an old man at sixty years of age, but still active in voice, and humor and command over

35

hundreds of loosely defined tribes. King Azar sat on a dais, covered in carpets, slightly dozing. Servants surrounded him, one fanned him, another held a tray should he require refreshments. He was expecting his caller but failed to act so.

Two guards at the door of the tent made way for his officer, who entered the tent, saluted, and approached Azar, bowing. The officer, speaking in Arabic, said, "King Azar, Queen Cleopatra of Egypt approaches and craves an audience with you" .Azar, also in Arabic, replied, "Oh no, she's found me at last. Oh well, it was only a matter of time, I suppose. I'm impressed by how much ground she's covered since and how many of my fellow kings has she bothered in the last few weeks, I wonder? Show the beggar Queen in, let's hear what she has to say at least. "The office bowed again before leaving and replied" As you command, sire. The officer saluted again, bowed and headed out of the tent.

Azar took a moment to try to look alert and give a severe expression change to haughtiness, as he heard Cleopatra and her advisers approaching the tent.

As Cleopatra ducked and entered the tent door. Azar switched to Greek "Queen Cleopatra. How honored I am to meet you, under such difficult circumstances for you". Cleopatra, stood just inside the doorway of the tent with her advisers and Appolodorus behind her, not bowing but quickly replying" Great King Azar, the honor is mine. It seems you have heard of my particular situation?"

Azar gestured for her to take the seat in front of him and clapped his hands for the cupbearer to pour him and her both drinks. There was little eye contact while she and he both drink at the same time. Azar finally looked straight at her and replied "Bad news has wings, my dear.Word reached me, but I admit the details are somewhat hazy. Naturally, I have a word of your progress in this land. My sincerest condolences for your discomforts, missing your beloved palace, no doubt, finishing with a nasty smile and adding 'I must ask...you were not actually ejected from your own palace?" Cleopatra replied quickly and defiantly, "Impossible. I would not have allowed it. I felt it best to leave while the minds of the people had been poisoned against me, by the foul whispering of my brother's people, the eunuch and the other ones. When my people realize they have been left with an impudent boy, controlled by those creatures, they will call out for my return".

Azar smiled and replied, "And when might this triumphant return take place?" Cleopatra, smiled in return" That is, as you must know, rather in your hands. There is no need for guile or untruths between us. I find myself currently short of an army and come to you for assistance, that's all". Azar smiled, then laughed slightly, "Is that how you put it?

You have, what, thirty men, sorry, men and women with you now. Saying you lack an army is possibly the understatement of the ages". Cleopatra, looked down at her hands, unfazed, she checked her nails and replied "This is only a temporary state of affairs. Whether I return this moon, next moon, or in twelve is irrelevant.

I will be queen, sole queen, once more, and those who have helped me along the way will be rewarded beyond their wildest expectations and those who stood in my path, naturally, will be put to death without mercy". Azar, smiled, "Fine words, my lady". Cleopatra smiled wryly" Tell me, my king, is this your palace? Where might I find my room for tonight?"

Azar again smiled sweetly," Palace? What need have I of a palace when I have the desert as my floor and the stars as my roof. What I need, I have, and that is twenty thousand men, horses, camels, and women, here, and all I have to do is click my fingers." To which Cleopatra replied, "I will give you palaces, horses, statues of gold, jewels for your women, and enough food for your men for a thousand years. What you do with your palaces is up to you. You may raze them to the ground if you prefer to sleep on the desert, of course. Who am I to deny a king his choice of bedchamber".

Azar looks hard at her, and she returned his gaze, unblinkingly. He sized her up and said,"I cannot deny I have long yearned to see the wonders of your cities. They are legendary for their beauty and splendor. Which is my palace to be then? One next to yours, so I may visit whenever I choose?" She smiled and Ignored the innuendo. "If you are the first to pledge your allegiance to me, you may have the pick of the lands of Cyrenaica and Nubia". Her advisers shift slightly behind her and look at each other.

She sensed this, flickered her eyes at them and continued, "I have many lands which I can bequeath to you. Our mother Nile blesses us with too much food to feed our nation, leaving us with simply too many riches to know what to do with. If you turn me away now, there may only be the scraps left to fight over when you come to join the fight, as surely you will. For why would you turn away the riches of Egypt? What fool would?"

Azar flinched at the word 'fool', and sat more upright and smoothed the folds in his tunic, carefully. "I seem to remember hearing something about your father, making similar pretty promises to some Romans. Let me think, how did that go again?"

Cleopatra seems to know what is coming, she looked discomposed but didn't know how to avoid the discussion.

King Azar went on...ah yes, that was it. He came petitioning to Gabinius, not even Caesar, Pompey or one of those, just some general. And... Oh yes, this is the good bit. Gabinius couldn't even be bothered to get off the toilet to greet your father!"

Azar laughs uproariously, and he is joined by his officers standing behind Cleopatra's people. Cleopatra and hers remain completely silent, waited for the mirth to die down. Azar wiped his eyes. "Come on, you have to admit, that's pretty funny. Great Pharaoh, Ptolemy the Piper or whichever one he was, begging help to get his beloved country back from his daughter, your sister right? To a man, on, the toilet. I can't remember who told me that, but I thank him now for that memory."

Cleopatra tried to interject, but he cut her off. "So you see, I have already more than exceeded expectations, receiving you in this dignified manner, and not in our privy tent. I hope you appreciate the gesture." Cleopatra was finally feeling the effects of the long trek, the sun and stress. Hot and tired, she replied angrily, "King Azar! I am not here to trifle with you! I have travelled long and far, and it is no hardship for me to suffer insults, slights, torments, sleepless nights, thirst, the accursed scorching Syrian sun or otherwise!

The only people who these delays inconvenience are the people of Egypt!" Azar spoke soothingly, as to young daughter, no longer laughing, "Come now, dear queenling. I meant no offense! There's no need for that pretty little face to look so cross. I just couldn't resist recounting that memory. No-one around me here has a sense of humor, I'm sad to say. We are on the whole a dour lot, that one especially." Cleopatra was not mollified and up and started pacing then turned to glare at Azar. Before she could say anything, Azar spoke carefully" Actually, believe it or not, I have kept myself informed of your country's politics, and watched your family's antics with great interest. I will regret saying this, no doubt, but I've always felt you were the right 'man' for the job, so to speak. I can't deny I had even hoped for an auspicious marriage, beneficial to both our peoples, one day, but then you Ptolemies have always had a penchant for marrying one another, which instead counts me out".

Cleopatra stared "I do not foresee the marriage to my brother being a particularly long-lived one. However, I offer no such terms. My offer of lands is adequate. Unless you feel I should offer the first choice to someone else of course." King Azar smiled "Well, let's see who else joins the fight, shall we?"

Cleopatra paused, looked directly into his eyes and carefully said," You will fight with me?" Azar picked at a grape skin and replied, "I'm sensing my army grows fat and idle and is in good need of a run-around. I will help you negotiate with the other Kings, those who don't spit on my name, that is. I could never resist a pretty nose. I wouldn't want to put yours out of joint.

Cleopatra finally sat down by the dais and taking the glass off the server replied with a small smile, "I fail to see how my nose bears any relevance on the future of Egypt." Azar laughed" No, I didn't think you would. Don't worry, little Queen. You will come to understand us and our rough ways out here.

A few more weeks on that saddle of yours and we'll have your shapely behind toughened up nicely".

Cleopatra forced a small smile, "First my nose, now my behind? I shall have to consult my advisers on which part of your anatomy I should compliment, for at present I am at a loss for words. "Azar chuckled" Touche, my lady. You're a hotheaded little thing, but I think we're going to get on just fine." Azar and Cleopatra smile at one another and clinked their glasses together. Dancing boys entertained in the fading firelight as they stopped talking, allowing Cleopatra to relax for the first time since she had fled. She had finally found a place to call a temporary home and an army.

The next day, late in the evening, after a very full sleep, she finally woke up in her tent. A hundred tents were set up around a central area, with campfires burning as the evening supper of goat meat and camel milk was prepared. Many more tents and tribes would join them, soon. Her staff was sitting around the fire, some were making food, others are just sitting or lying about. Cleopatra opened the tent flap and came out, wrapped in a shawl, looking tired and bleary and hung over. Her advisers and Apollodorus look at each other knowingly and get up to greet her. Cleopatra rubbed her head and said," what happened?" Diogenes got up "Good evening, O Majesty. We trust you slept well?" There was some tittering within the camp, but Cleopatra seems oblivious to it. Cleopatra put her hand to her temples and rubbed them "I was with Azar... We were discussing whether to approach other local kings and then... I woke up here. How did I get back here?". Appolodorus got up and spoke" That was my honor, my Queen. You appeared, um, desirous of some assistance". Cleopatra looked at him, and half joking said, "Carrying me again, were you, Appolodorus?

Let's not make a habit of that, shall we." Appolodorus put his head down and replied: "No, Majesty. "He bowed but smiled to himself . Cleopatra moves forward to sit down by the fire, and her advisers struggle to throw down their cloaks for her, but she ignores them and merely sat on the ground, staring into the light and said, "So, it seems we have the beginnings of our army if I remember right?" To which Jahi replied "Indeed, Majesty. You were most successful in that regard. It may have been your generous offer of Cyrenaica and Nubia that caused Azar to break out his finest wines for you." Cleopatra looked at him and replied, "Oh! You're not going to lecture me on that now, are you? I don't think I could bear it. At least I didn't agree to marry the old toad, so spare me you're haranguing. My head is about to explode." With that comment, she carefully got up and walked back, towards her tent, calling out painfully, "Charmion! is there nothing you can give me for the pain?" Charmion came running out of the tent, carrying a phial of liquid. She hurries over to Cleopatra and kneels on one knee to present her with the phial. Cleopatra took it and downed it in one gulp. Charmion stood beside her.

39

Cleopatra looked at her, "You warned me about this part of negotiating with kings and warlords. Prepare a concoction for me in advance next time, something that blocks the pain." Charmion looked at Iras, standing in the door of the tent, who just shrugged and smiled. Charmion turned back to Cleopatra "Of course, Majesty". Cleopatra did not seem to take that comment well and said "I wish I had brought my most exceptional chemist with us. His expertise is invaluable especially now!"

Later that night, Cleopatra in her tent conferred with her advisers, prepared their plans and talks with tribal leaders. Diogenes, standing next to her looking at a map, "We set up camp here during your...er.. discussions last night, Queen Cleopatra. Azar will be expecting us tomorrow, to finalize your next move. There was some talk of heading further into the desert towards Lake El Talgah, to gather other tribes. What are your thoughts on this?" Cleopatra stared a the map, thought carefully and replied, "I don't like it, but it does make sense to avoid the mountains. We need to gather support, little by little, from the desert leaders, and then gather at the lake, where we have water and fish. When the larger kingdoms see our army, they may choose to join us, or at worst, leave us alone".

Jahi, on the other side of the table, quickly replied, "Or attack, of course." She looked at him," We'll see. I intend to have an army 20,000 strong by the time we return to Egypt. Azar has promised me five thousand of his savages, and maybe more, depending on what we get from the desert. He attested to their great bravery, but also to their love of feasting and women, so I hope you have our coffers ready to keep them happy" Diogenes bowed, but frowned, she went on, "Not to mention how we are going to move this army to Egypt without raising the alarm in Alexandria. Ships would be preferable, but waters will be full of pirates. So, by land it is".

Jahi, always the pessimist replied" Nothing is impossible, but to proceed unheeded through Judaea would be nothing short of a miracle. We don't know whose service your brother has already bought. It may be wise to dispatch some of Azar's men as scouts to scout ahead". Cleopatra took a sip of water

" Agreed. I'll discuss that with Azar now. Who knows how long it will take to get my army rallied? Finally, find favor with Azar of all people, I don't know how the Ptolemies have come to this."

Diogenes gave her a smile and on a more positive not said" He may not be noble or descended from your ancestors, O'Queen, but maybe this is only to your benefit, given your family's, um, history for fratricide and so on. In my opinion, finding Azar has been the best thing for you,he is a thug, yes, but honest, straight-talking and, most importantly, has a loyal army that will follow him, and now you, to the end". Cleopatra picked up a coin, holding the map in place and looking at it added, "Aided by a little coin, along the way. "I'm afraid that goes without saying, majesty. Jahi said. Cleopatra Sighed "Well, let's get on with it. My head is pounding, but now I have caught the scent of action, I will follow it with all my determination. Azar will take us back to Alexandria. I have to believe that". And with that comment, the meeting broke up.

Cleopatra stood at the back of the tent, besides Azar. Her advisers behind her, the tent ahead is filled with desert leaders, loyal somewhat to Azar, all in desert attire, all sitting on carpets and cushions. The men talked loudly among themselves, with Cleopatra and Azar looking around the group. Azar nodded over to a seated man remarked, "I told you we'd get Bashaz". Cleopatra cut in, "And this is a good thing?" Azar smiled" Well, it is if you like your enemies to be tortured brutally and their skin used as interesting headgear". Cleopatra looked at him somewhat in alarm "What? We have such a man, leader, among our number?"

Azar whispered back, "Oh don't worry about it, little Queen. It's not going to come to that. It's good to have his revolting reputation preceding your army though." Cleopatra whispered back" That's... great tidings...I suppose". Azar faced her "Right! Are you ready for your rallying cry? All the ones you've done before were just practicing for this one. Most of these kings, sheiks and clansmen are brutes.

Brutes with horses, men and weapons, but lacking in the finer sensibilities. They are not used to little queens telling them what to do. You have to give them a reason to follow you." Cleopatra looked about and added, "I can do that. Come with me. I want you beside me." They moved forward to the front of the crowd of murmuring men. Azar smiled and followed Cleopatra to the front of the gathering. Eyes follow her as she walked proudly, though them, in simple but regal attire. Finally, coming to stand, the chatter went quiet. She spoke in Syrian, her Aunt's language and one of seven languages that she used. Cleopatra now had their attention" Great leaders of the endless desert. You have come here, of your own accord, leaving behind your daily existences, to enter a new world. An extraordinary world, of beauty, knowledge and wealth.

Someone butted in, "Who cares about knowledge? I just like my women beautiful!". Someone else laughed and hinted "Wealth isn't bad either!" There were laughter and chatter among the group, which Azar clucked to silence. Cleopatra went on, "For the short time of sacrifice I ask of you, you and your descendants will have a share in Egypt's bounty". There was more chatter, though people are starting to look keen. Cleopatra continued on"

You treasure the sun, the moon and the stars in the desert. Imagine how they look in a new sky, a sky that is yours, and your sons' and daughters' after you. A sky under which you sit, served the most exceptional food and wine, surrounded by your wealth and glory. All this will be yours, in return for restoring my kingdom to me"? Another leader spoke

41

up" And women, we get new women too? "She silenced the crowd with her stern look at the last speaker and raised her hand. "Wine, food, women, and wealth are nice. But what of glory, honor? I know these mean the same to you as they do to me, for we are all rulers, chosen by the gods to lead our people. Your people, they need you to provide for them, to do what's best for them, and I need you so I can do the same for my people". She raised her voice, "Join me now, fight with me, and I will share with you the glory of the ancient land of Egypt, share the knowledge of thousands of years, and grant you the blessings of our gods, that will bring you and future generations everlasting life! Together, we will crush our enemies!" She looked around and sees the effect on the men. Something more was needed, from the looks on their faces's so she quickly added as she rolled her eyes, "And I'll pay you a lot of money!" An a massive cry of approval from the crowd, the wine began to flow.

In the aftermath, Azar and Cleopatra conferred again. Azar whispered into her ear" That was all you really needed to say". She whispered back quickly, "I know! What a waste of words but I have to stay here at least until I know who will win the war between Caesar and Pompey, and who knows, the Romans may help me also. So if these men stay till then, I can then attack Egypt. Ah, my mouth is as dry as a bone after all that talk. How about some of that wine you tried to kill me with the first time we met? I have grown a taste for it." They smile at each other as they were handed drinks, and left the leaders group to their merrymaking of wine, dancing boys and meat.

46 BC. The Royal Barge near Temple of Horus.

The Royal barge and the ships that followed behind it sailed onward down the Nile. The mid-afternoon sun made the dryness and heat, unbearable for some of those in the rice fields near the river. Many a worker, slept under the trees, only to wake up a few hours later and complete their work in the cooler air. Caesar sat with Cleopatra on the deck. Fanned and cooled by a dozen servants. The Nile also gave a reprieve to the heat. Caesar carefully speared some olives and took yet another glass of wine before he spoke, "By the Gods, you had the strength to work the Arabs into an army.

Well done! I'm not sure that I could have done the same. They are a wild and uncouth bunch." Cleopatra smiled, thinking back to those desert times, not so far gone and changed the subject. "Caesar you had me worried, no word of you, of your sickness or victory." Caesar replied, "Well, there were times when I thought I was finished. After recovering from my infliction, we hurried to Greece to a large valley with a field called Pharsalus. There, both Pompey and I did hesitate to fight. After all, we were both Roman, he had married my daughter, and we were once both friends, but all had changed. Finally, it happened. Pompey won the first battle, his man's gloried in their so-called victory, relaxed their guard, after all, they outnumbered us three to one. But, I know the way of fighting and pulled out one of my trick cards and took the day". He smiles reflected his pride even though he killed many a Roman that day.

47 BC. Summer, Greece, Parasalus.

Caesar sat on his horse with the other generals overlooking the fighting from a nearby hilltop. Antony remarked about Pompay "He loves a fight does he not? But we must put a quick end to this fight". Caesar replied," Yes, you are right, but before the battle starts, I will talk to my men." Caesar confronted his troops and called out to them." As before in Gaul we suffered and won, now we have suffered again, but as before, we will win again! Have I, your 'father', ever let you down?" Thousands of men cheer their loyal support and scream out. 'No!" .Caesar replied to their cry. " Then let the end begin!" Caesar then told Sapinus. "Take one thousand of our cavalry from their hidden place and attack his left flanked horses." Tullius, overhearing said "Attack, Pompey's seven thousand riders with our one thousand?!" Caesar looked at him, impatiently, "They will panic and be squashed like ripe grapes, and we will win the day or be damned." Sapinus rode off with a parting comment, "Let this start be the end!"

There was a significant distance between the two armies. Pompey ordered his men not to charge, but to wait until Caesar's legions came into close quarters. Caesar's men advanced carefully then both sides engage. Pompey's legions took the attack aggressively, due to their deep formations and having more men. Pompey then ordered his cavalry to attack Caesar's left flank and as expected, they successfully push back Caesar's left flank cavalry until suddenly seemingly out of nowhere, Caesar's hidden fourth line of horsemen, hidden in the woods, joined in, and thrust at Pompey's cavalry, squeezing Pompey's Calvary on both sides, causing general panic and turning them to flight.

After observing his cavalry routing, Pompey retreated to his camp and left his troops to their own devices, ordering the garrison to defend camp as he gathered his family, loaded up gold, and threw off his general's cloak and fled to Egypt by boat. Later that evening in Caesar's tent, Antony, attended by a doctor who treated an arrow wound, remarked, "That was a very close fight, my friend." Caesar replied, "Yes, it was." Antony went on," What will you do about the surrender of his generals, Brutus, Cassius, and about Pompay, they said that he fled the field?".

Caesar studied his feet, then replied, "I fear he has fled to Egypt to seek the help of Cleopatra and her brother. As for Brutus and Cassius, well, they are family, I will pardon them both. Antony did not smile and for once, and made no humorous reply but asked, "Very generous of you. So, what do you wish to do now, return to Rome in splendor or pursue Pompey?" Caesar replied "I will pardon his troops and send them to Gaul and half our troops back to hold Rome and the other half for Egypt with ourselves. We'll use Pompey's ships, as he has no further use for them! I need to stop Pompey from hiring more Egyptian military and counter-attacking me".

46 BC. The Royal Barge near Philae.

Cleopatra suddenly jumped up from the cushions and ran to the ship's railing and pointed at the temples, as they floated by. "Oh! It's the 'Island of Philae' with the 'Temple of Isis and Osiris!'.

We must stop here!" As soon as they docked, she prayed to Isis thanking her for her kind intervention. Caesar joined her later and sat next to her on a stone bench in the shade. "Why did they build this temple in the middle of the river?" "There are several reasons, my love, she replied. One is that the shadow of the south and the sun of the north meet right here in the river.

Thus, it's also the border of our land and the lands of Nubia. This temple is the place where Osiris was buried, thus Isis, my protector also dwells here.

It was she that came to me when I was bitten, and all that has come to pass since then is as she foretold". Caesar, dusted the dirt from his tunic and looked at her in admiration, then thinking back, asked, "who built your camp and why at El Talqar lake? "Cleopatra smiled and said "You are not the only one to consider logistics. The lake was far enough from Egypt and close enough to Roman control territory if needed. The waters of the lake fed and watered us for sixteen months. It was also a place where the tribes could gather." As she talked, she thought back to those rough times in the desert.

49-48 BC. Winter, Syrian Desert.

Scattered around were hundreds of tents, with and men cooking. Winter in the desert was more comfortable than summer, but fires had to be tended. With so many camels, over twenty-thousand, there was plenty of dry dung to burn and use for cooking and keeping warm. Lake El Talqar provided water for the thousands of camels, horses, goats that the various tribes brought with them.

Wearing new soft sheepskin coats and boots, Cleopatra walked through the camp, deliberately taking the long way towards the cave in the cliffs nearby, where they washed, in order to show she was one with them all and not afraid, even as a woman, along with Charmion and Iras, who are both looking quite nervous. Men huddled around fires, playing dice, and looked up to see Cleopatra passed them, and nodded their acknowledgement. Charmion complained, "must we walk through the camp like this?" Cleopatra looked shocked "What! You'd have me brave these soldiers alone?" Charmion rushed to correct herself and looking nervously around, "Not at all, Cleo, that's not what I meant! I just meant, couldn't you have Diogenes or Jahi with you or even Appolodorus? I don't think this is a place for ladies".

Cleopatra looked at her, "That's exactly why we're doing this. I want to show these desert barbarians that we women are not afraid of them. It's been a hard thing to get their respect, as it is". Iras, walking behind them, also was not comfortable. "I see she said" that makes sense Cleo, but must they smell quite so bad? I do wish we were back in our tent, upwind of this camp. Haven't they heard of proper toilets"!

As she wrinkled her nose. Cleopatra smiled "I expect there's not a lot of our ways that they have heard of. How many of them do you see reading scrolls or practicing their languages? However that's not what I need these men for. They are here to fight, to attack, to kill, essentially". Iras, not looking assured replied, "True, Cleo. I just hope they remember who it is they are supposed to kill. You don't think they'll turn on us in our sleep?" Cleopatra walked on "Actually, no I don't. They have proved quite loyal to me, at least Azar, so far. Yesterday a fight broke out between two clan leaders, and Diogenes stepped in to break it up. I thought they were going to butcher him on sight, but they immediately stopped, apologized, and scuttled back to their tents! It seems miracles can happen". Charmoin looking happy, "That is good news! I mean that they haven't tried to kill any of us yet."

"Here we are," said Charmion. They entered the huge cavern where the Royal Guards waited for them. The women quickly disrobed and washed quickly, in the cold air. Feeling most refreshed, Cleopatra, sat still on a rock, while Iris and Charmion dressed her with a simple dress, warm fleece coat and fur-lined boots.

Next, Charmion applied a new face powder. "What is in this new powder?" Cleopatra asked. Charmion smiled," This will protect your face from the harsh sunlight. It's calcite powder, senator, resin, wax, fresh balanos oil, Cyprus grass, and a bit of camel's milk". "Hand me the mirror, Iris" Cleopatra asked. Iris passed her the ivory-handled mirror. Cleopatra stared carefully into the mirror. "My face is as dark as a camel driver's wife" she complained!

Charmion laughed "it's the cavern, the light is poor in here, but you have been under this sun for some time now. Not to worry, this cream will help". The talk turned to men. "What about you", asked Cleopatra, looking at Iris. Have any of these men... you know...tried it on with you? Iris fainted shock" I would not know, Cleo"! Cleopatra laughed, "Of course you wouldn't, Iras. So when Charmion saw you coming out of Jahi's tent the other night, you were just bringing him some honey water out of concern for his health?" Iras looks shocked and embarrassed for a second, then they all laughed, like friends, the sound echoing off the walls. Cleopatra, still smiling asked "Don't imagine I have changed that much since you first started serving me, ladies. We were friends were we not? I may have been busier since father died, becoming a queen at last, but I am still human!" Then looking conspiratorial added "But that's a secret between you both and me and to this bunch, let's try to preserve the fantasy".

Iras raised an eyebrow "fantasy?" Cleopatra said. "That I am a goddess!' She laughed! Cleopatra`s mood turned inward. "I miss the markets in Alexandria, the smells and flowers. Iris, do you miss your home?" Iris reflected a bit, then replied "no, not really.

There is no one left to miss in Kush. My mother died in Meroe when I was young. She, as you know was related to Candace of Mereo, and left me money for my education, plus my father was a gold merchant before he died. I loved to see what he had to sell. He used to show me, gold dust, gold bracelets and more. I was lucky that he had left orders for me to be educated in Alexandria in the finer ways and to finally serve you. I'm happy with my life, even here!" Cleopatra smiled "I'm lucky to have you both as my maids. And what about you, Charmion?"

Charmion smiled as she folded the towels and put the cosmetics away in the case. "You know my circumstances" she replied. "Yes, that's true but do you miss Cyprus?" Cleopatra asked. Charmion paused and thought aloud, "Well, at times I do miss the dry hills and olive trees. My family grew olive trees in the central mountains. We stored them in huge iron pots, then sold them when business came calling. It's those olives that brought me to Alexandria and finally to you!

It's the education that my grandmother gave me that made me interested in medicine and food, saying 'someday, we will all become famous, just because of olives!" They all laughed together!

47

47 BC. Spring time, Syrian Desert.

A few months later, the tribal leaders gathered, standing, looking agitated in King Azar's tent. There was a lot of chatter along the lines of "We're not going any further and 'I don't want any part of this anymore', 'You will lead us to certain death'. And some deemed to desert her cause.

Azar stood in the middle of them, shouting in Arabic for them to calm down, be quiet, all will be well. Cleopatra and Iras entered into the confusion, and as they caught sight of her, moved towards her with the same chants. Her advisers were already there and moved to block them from her, and eventually, the tribe leaders calm down enough for conversation. Cleopatra looked at her advisors, "What is the meaning of this? Is it more money they want?" Diogenes replied "No, my lady. It seems a tribal leader named 'Soltan' sent his own scout south towards the border of Egypt, and reports your brother has gathered forces, and they prepare to move over the Nile, towards Palusium".

Cleopatra looked shocked, "What! Has anyone joined him beside the army?" "That's unclear as yet, though some Roman envoys were also spotted in Alexandria", he replied. Cleopatra, now horrified "We are done for! How are we going to defeat them, especially if they have Romans reporting to them?" Jahi then spoke up, "That is the general gist of these gentleman's concerns,it seems". They are also aware of this situation. Cleopatra looked at Azar, desperately, "What will it take for them to stay with me?"

Azar, looking at the assembled throng asked them in Arabic" The little Queen asks what else you thieves want from her, to continue with her on her journey home. More shouting and gesticulating, with cries of "money, a thousand virgins, more land, wine, two thousand camels". Eventually, they quieted down, and Azar said to her." I would not listen to these scoundrels, little Queen, or bend to any more demands. You have promised to reward them handsomely. They had just not thought the need to fight. I say let them leave if they want. My men are strong, and if we move fast towards Judea, we may yet gather others, not these weak-bellied scum. It seems they want a sign from their god or gods, but I don't know what kind".

Cleopatra thought a bit then replied "I see. I don't suppose they think I'm a god, then?" Azar smiled "Sadly, no". Cleopatra looked around the tent and replied quietly, "Too bad... this is ill news indeed. I need some time to think". Cleopatra agitated, turns to walk out of the tent, and her advisers scuttled to follow her, and the tumult starts up again, with Azar being left to fend off the petitioners.

Cleopatra walked fast out of the tent, flanked by her advisers, with Charmion and Iras close behind her. She was apparently upset and was fiddling with her attire. Diogenes finally caught up with her, "My lady?"

48

Cleopatra was more than agitated, "My lady what? What are you going to say that is actually of any use? My filthy brother tramping up north towards us, and he's got the real Egyptian army behind him, which is more convincing than what we have here. Given the prospect of a full Egyptian army coming their way, I couldn't really blame them if they take flight. Is there nothing we can do? "Is there"?" she looked at him angrily. Diogenes murmured quietly "No, my lady." "I thought not", she fired back. "So, if you've got nothing useful to say, I want to be left alone. No, actually, Iras come with me, I need you". She stormed off, leaving her advisers shocked and worried, but with Iras running along after her. Iras ran to catch up with her fast pace, "How can I assist, my Queen?"

Cleopatra clenched her teeth and replied," Gather minimal supplies and a couple of camels and come with me. I have no appetite for this right now. Some of these men will no doubt leave now, some will stay. I would rather not be here when all this unfolds. Diogenes, Jahi and Azar can deal with it." "But, where will we go?" Iras said. Cleopatra looked straight ahead" Just... away, into the desert. We will stay the night. I need some peace and space to arrange my thoughts. I am always surrounded by these ruffians, by advice, counsel, meetings, talking... just endless... talking. For once, I just want to be alone. Make haste and see to it... Please!"

Then, turning to Charmion "Bring Iras and Apollodorus. No one else". Charmion gave a quick bow as best she could at such a pace "Yes, O Queen. At once" They parted ways, walking off into the camp.

An hours ride away, Charmion, Iras, Apollodorus and Cleopatra sat by a campfire in the desert, with a tent in the background Charmion looked at Cleopatra with concern. Appolodorus tending to the fire, "Would you like me to prepare your bed, my Queen? I am concerned you are tired from the journey". Cleopatra vacantly replied, "No, thank you, Appolodorus. I don't feel tired. I just feel.. lost".

Iras, ever simple, replied "We're not lost, are we... O Queen?" Cleopatra gave her a sweet look and said, "Not like that, for goodness' sake. We're only half a day's ride from a camp of thousands of men. They probably all know where we are anyway. I imagine Diogenes will have had us followed. He fusses like an old woman." Appolodorus poked at the fire again "Still, majesty, you must prepare for the day ahead. Please allow me to make you comfortable.

"Cleopatra moved to get up, "Gods! I'm surrounded by fussers! Why can't you just let me be? We may be sat by a fire in the middle of nowhere, but I am still your queen..." then, looking vacant again, and then talking to herself... "Aren't I?" "Yes, Queen", they all said, sensing together that all was not well. Cleopatra looked at them all, smiled fondly and said, "Look at you... my loyal subjects. What few I have left. Who am I really, when I take off the headdress and sit on this hard ground, not on my royal throne? What am I? I could die out here... quickly. And what would be left of me, the last queen of Egypt? How fast would the vultures pick my bones clean?"

Who would tell how queen Cleopatra met her noble end." Iras and Appolodorus only look at each other and maintained their silence. She continued, "Don't worry about me, I'm not dying, not today, but I am going for a walk.

Appolodorus suddenly got up in panic "But it is the black of night, my Queen! I will come with you!" Cleopatra spoke firmly and with some anger said, "You will not. You will leave me be. Stay here, and watch out for me, if you must. That's an order!" Then, picking up a torch out of the fire, she straightened up, and strolled away into the dark desert night, leaving everyone else wondering what to do.

Cleopatra's face was lit up by the torch she carried into the very black night. She is walked slowly, a blank expression on her face, thinking nothing, just walking, up one sand dune and down another. Eventually, she comes to a stop, stood and looked ahead, suddenly she screams, a small scorpion has struck her foot, poison was seeping in.

Appolodorus snapped his head up, "Did you hear that! Screams in the night?" Iras stood up, "Find her quickly!" They followed her tracks and finally found her fallen in the sand, sweating, rolling in pain, delirious with fever, they saw the scorpion bite. Quickly, Appolodorus carried her carefully back to the tent. Charmain shouted to Iras, "Get the medicine box and take out the Gastrodia root, cinnamon oil, green figs, wax, and marrow, mixed and ready quickly and apply it to her foot!

Cleopatra went into a dreaming state, and in her mind, she talked saw Isis, her Goddess protector.

Cleopatra dreamt on and spoke to Isis, "I knew I would find you here." Isis herself glowed from a bush that burned. Her voice was distorted, made to sounds sweet but almost non-human. Isis replied," Come, child, look upon me". Cleopatra straightened her head and looked up and said, "Can it really be you, Great Mother, Isis?" Isis smiled at her and replied, "Who better to comfort you now, in your time of the greatest need?" Cleopatra whimpered in her sleep and replied: "Forgive me". Isis looked down at her". Forgive you... for what? Cleopatra stuttered "I...I... I have let you down in so many ways. I call myself after you, yet I have not worshipped you as I should. "Isis said" And I have been with you all the time. My strength has returned, thanks to your belief. I am nourished by your love. For this I am grateful".

Cleopatra bowed her head, crying, shaking her head, "I married my brother as you did, yet I love him not and do not wish to have a Pharaoh by him, as I should. And here I am, alone in the desert, not fit to be a queen..."Isis touched her head

"Do you think you are the first mortal to attempt to be me, to use my name as their own? I know humans, I know you are flawed, weak, and changeable."

This concerns me not. So, why do you think I am here?" Cleopatra shivered in her sleep and replied in her dream, looking afraid "I fear you may not be here. I have been so lost and afraid, and my mind may be playing tricks with me. I fear that if it were really you, you would judge me here and now, and you would find me wanting. Isis smiled a mother's smile and replied softly, "No, child. I am not here to judge you. I am here to show you the way. What you then do, is up to you. Only you can judge yourself." Cleopatra dried her tears with one hand "The way? The way back to Alexandria?" Isis replied, "Yes, child".

Cleopatra wondered aloud, "How to rid myself of my brother... to defeat his army?" Isis looked stern "I do not condone the murder of your brother. My dearest desire is to preserve the lives of my children. My sorrow fills the rivers. Each of my tears waters your fields. My grief has made you rich and powerful."

Cleopatra bowed her head again" I know, great mother. For your child Horus I weep too. We are thankful for your bounty... but my brother seeks to destroy me!". Isis looked down at her sternly"

There is a way, that you may return to lead your people, to bring Egypt back to the true way, to shed no blood in my name, and to gain a powerful alliance that will strengthen both your and my power.

We will bring a mother's love for the land... and in your home". Cleopatra looked up quickly, "I am to be a mother?" Isis smiled again" Oh yes, child. And what a mother you will be. A noble lioness, mother to the most royal lion cub." Cleopatra smiled, tears in her eyes and replied: "Show me how!" Isis seemed to be disappearing before her eyes "I believe you are ready, you shall have your throne by your next birthday".

Cleopatra stood up, feeling better by the second "You've seen me lose my home, my life and my country, and yet you are here to lead me. I will go wherever you take me, great Isis, mother of all." Isis came closer to her, now almost gone and replaced with a glow "No more need for words. Come here, child." Cleopatra walked towards Isis, getting subsumed into the glow that surrounds her. They embrace, as a mother and a child. Then Isis took Cleopatra's face in her hands and looks straight at her. Cleopatra arches her head back and gives out a silent cry; finally, she dreams a falcon eating the scorpion and flying off, a good Omen.

It was two mornings later, early morning. Appolodorus and Charmion slept by the embers of the fire, clothed, but with their arms around each other. They slowly wake up and look up, and quickly pull themselves together, stood up and bowed. Cleopatra stood

51

regally, looking confident renewed, smiled at them, as she said, "I trust you had a good night, my loyal subjects? Charmion quickly looked at the ground in embarrassment. "A thousand apologies, my Queen.

We fell asleep while we waited for you to recover. Appolodorus mumbled something and bowed with a quick "Yes, my Queen". Cleopatra looked at them both, "It looks like you had a good time anyway. Probably not quite as good as I did though."

Charmion looked confused and curious. "My lady?" Cleopatra moved back towards the tent, "I have seen a good omen. No time to waste now. Get this packed up. I want to return to the camp before noon," she shouted over her shoulder. I have a country to win back!" Charmion and Appolodorus shared a glance, and then hasten to pack up the things. They made their way back to the main camp. No one was particularly surprised to see them saunter into camp but everyone noticed Cleopatra's mood had changed for the better. Later that night in a more comfortable bed, she slept a full and sound sleep.

47 BC. Summer, Syrian Desert.

The spring turned to the hot summers where even the tents did not keep one cool. Many animals and men spent time near the lake, washing and trying to stay cool. Weeks turned into months as they trained and slept. Cleopatra would not move until all the men had arrived and she was sure of they're training. Many men were all bluster and had never seen a real battle or killed anyone in anger. She wanted to make sure they could hold their own. One day late in the summer, Azar met her and asked directly "My Princess, we have used all the money made from the sale of your pearls. Now, if we are to keep these men, we will need more food and money from you, can you provide that?" Cleopatra called Iras over, "Get my pearls". Iras went over to her tent and soon came back with a long string of pearls. Cleopatra took them and gave them to Azar, "Spend well, my friend, for those are the last, and if more is needed, I have none, so make it last." Azar juggled the pearls and said, "I am sure we will see more after we dispose of your brother."

She looked at him and replied, "That day had better come soon. Now if no one objects, I would like to celebrate my twenty-first birthday! Azar, where is the wine!" Later, they retired to their tents and beds. The female Guards outside of the front of the tent chatted not far from Cleopatra's tent. As the stars circled overhead in a moonless night, a shadow crept to the back of her tent, cut a quick hole near the bottom of it and crawled in. It was quiet, pitch black in the tent and hard to see who was sleeping where but the figure went for the sleeping head in the centre of the group.

As he moved like a snake, past the outer body, Appolodorus, who slept lightly, grabbed the assassin's foot as he passed by, crying out, "Assassin has entered! "Guards, guards! I've got him. Let me have the honor of killing him!" The guards rush in and overpower the assassin and hauled him upright and held his hands behind him. Cleopatra sat upright, then stood up and seeing the situation said "Don't kill him! Bind him, I will deal with him personally in the morning. The prisoner was bound and led out by guards. Cleopatra then looked at her guards for that night. "You four guards will find something else to do, such collecting camel dung for the fires. You are lucky I don"t have you all executed".

The guards quickly apologized, bowed profusely and left in haste.

Very early the next day, the prisoner was led out, in front of her army, they wait to see what she would do while pelting him with garbage food and stones. Cleopatra arrived and walked into their midst, with a sword from one of her guards and went over and stood behind the prisoner. Azar watches from nearby as with other leaders. She lifted the sword and said, "Isis, this is my sacrifice to you!" and with those words, she killed him with a sword plunge to the back of the neck. He fell onto the dirt where he lay twitching

53

until someone dug a hole for him. Later in Azar's tent, Azar looked at Cleopatra and smiled "I know now these ruffians will follow you now. They know now that you are not just a pretty faced queen but also can kill". Cleopatra looked back and said slyly, "That sounds to me as if you had underestimated me, Azar". He nodded, smiled and replied, "Maybe I did, maybe I did". Cleopatra helped herself to some water and stated, "I gave the assassin what he deserved and now the men who have given me their oath to follow me, understand that I will kill or be killed, just as they may". Diogenes, her teacher, remarked from a corner of the tent" And how merciful, my Queen, you have been called upon to dispense judgment and done well."

Azar flattered her even more by adding, "Truly you have the makings of a perfect leader". Cleopatra chewed on some fresh goat meet and replied to all in a matter-of-fact tone 'What can I say. All we need is some good news... such as my sweet brother having choked to death on one of his toys". Azar spat out a pip and quipped "I fear it may not be that simple, Cleopatra." No, it is never easy is it, she snapped back" But with the gods and this army behind me, I feel I have earned my place on the throne again. It is your job to help me get there!"

Diogenes and Cleopatra watched the training of the tribesmen. "They are coming together as a force now" she remarked`. "Yes" Replied Diogenes, "they are ready". Cleopatra looked at the horsemen, "I may have misjudged these people. Someday they may become a force to deal with". Jahi smiled "that may happen but not today".

47 BC. Fall Time, Syrian Desert.

Finally, fall came, with colder days and nights and storms. Cleopatra and her advisors along with Azar talked about the time to move on Egypt. Some men had already left and been nomadic, they tired of being in one place.

Suddenly, there was the sound of a kerfuffle outside the tent. Jahi looked up in alarm, and stepped out of the tent, while Cleopatra and the ladies gathered together and stared towards the door opening.

As suddenly, a Roman messenger burst through the tent door, with his hands held behind his back by one of her Royal Guards. Cleopatra moved backwards and asked "What is the meaning of this? Who is this Roman?" A Royal Guard replied, "He says he's Roman messenger from Egypt." Cleopatra looked at the messenger, "What is your message? Who sent you? Release him."! The messenger shook himself free and handed her a message. She read the letter. Shocked, she looked up at the messenger. "Caesar is in Alexandria? What of Pompey?"

"The messenger quickly replied, "Pompey is dead by your brother's orders, Great Queen, Caesar arrived October 12th, and he requests your presence".

Cleopatra, angry, harshly asked, "You are telling me that Caesar, is in my palace, and is ordering me to come back!" The messenger looked nervous and shifted from one foot to the other, "Yes, Queen...he has also ordered your brother Ptolemy and sister to come to him. Caesar's wish is to oversee a parlay between you and the boy, Ptolemy, to secure peace in Egypt and a bring a resolution to your conflict".

Azar sarcastically noted. "Great, so, no fighting then?" Jahi moved towards Cleopatra, "Queen Cleopatra, this may be a...". Angrily, she cut him off "Silence! No-one speaks!"

She started to walk around. Everyone stood quietly and watched her. Finally she said "Caesar will guarantee my safe passage into Alexandria?" The messenger looked unsure 'O Queen... he...he didn't say exactly, but, he said you would be safe in Alexandria, with him. He didn't say anything about coming into the city."

Jahi jumped in, "Ha. It's a trap! His words give him away. No guarantee of safe passage means we are free to be butchered just before the Palace walls!" Azar`s face flushed with excitement "Good! So we do get to fight then"! Cleopatra stamped the carpet in anger" I said, silence!" She paused, placed her hands on her temples then said, "Tell Caesar. I accept his invitation. Tell him I will travel with my army until the sight of Pelusium, where we will make camp, and I will continue on to the Palace. My army is not to be approached or harmed in any way by his army."

The messenger exhaled and relieved replied "Yes, O Queen. I will tell him. He will be most... er, pleased". May I take my leave now?" The messenger looked for approval to leave. Jahi nodded.

A guard took the messenger out of the tent. Diogenes and Jahi look questioning at Cleopatra. While everyone stared at each other. Cleopatra burst into a huge smile, "Don't you see? Can't you see what's happened?" Diogenes spoke finally". You believe what Caesar has said?" Cleopatra nodded "I believe 'Uncle' Gaius Julius Caesar', wants to talk and will not harm me." Jahi was not convinced" But what are his goals? Caesar is positioned in your palace, with your brother is still in Pelusium, and we may still be intercepted by his forces before reaching the Nile!" Cleopatra gave a hollow laugh "I have no choice, if I stay here I will be left out of any deal making." Diogenes raised his eyebrows. "Pardon, my Queen, but you wish to make an...alliance with Caesar?"

She tossed her hair and with some sarcasm, "No, the thought hadn't crossed my mind at all! What do you think? With Caesar and Rome on my side, the game is over. I know his weaknesses, women, power and no male child. All I need to do is charm him with my words and my love-giving and produce a boy! My poor brother, how he will curse the gods that he was not born a beautiful woman, to best me now and my sister who has the brains of her father and will not impress him at all".

Jahi and Diogenes looked unsure, then the realization dawned on them. Diogenes grinned "So, you wish to make an, um, alliance!"

Cleopatra rolled her eyes in exasperation, "Give me patience! Get out, you old women, and get ready for tomorrow's journey. Do something useful for once. Apollodorus, you know what to do". Appolodorus nodded as he left, "Yes O'Queen". Azar turned from the door and said more respectfully, "I'm just glad you are to be Queen again. Just don't forget to pay me before you play house with this Roman." She smiled "Of course, old friend. You have proved to be a true friend this last year, and you did find me an army, and I will not forget that". "And just how will you get into the palace?" Azar asked, your brother will have guards on the lookout for you". Cleopatra grinned "The same way I got out. Get ready, we move south tomorrow!" Everyone looks carefully at Cleopatra, each with their own unspoken thoughts.

The men left. As evening fell, the tent was prepared for sleeping with carpets, bedding, cushions lining the floor and with small pots of fire to light the inside. Cleopatra looked at her maids. "Oh, this is your time now, girls! You are going to make me perfect. I want to dazzle him, enchant him, win him with a little love potent.

I will show him that I am the only one Egypt needs, the only queen for Rome also!" Charmion replied, "You will be, my lady. He will love you from the moment he sees you". Cleopatra laid down with her face upwards, thinking. "Ahhh, this is all falling into place. Mother Isis has made it so. My brother will be gone, Caesar will give me his blessing... and his son. I know it will be so." Charmion looked at her "But he is so old, can you be sure he can sire a son?" Cleopatra grinned, "You are right. Well, I am fertile like the Nile, tonight. Bring Appolodorus to me now, blindfolded and tell him nothing. I will take no chances with Caesar".

Soon after, Appolodorus arrived at the maid's tent, to be greeted by Charmion. Once bid inside, she ordered him to disrobe. Appolodorus replied, "I must prepare for our leaving and do not need a bath or food right now and why by you!?" Charmion clutched his arm and ordered him to obey and strip "Your Queen commands so". Since she was serious, he allowed both Charmion and Iras to wash his body and anoint it with fragrances. Then once finished, blindfolded him. Appolodorus finally asked, "Why all this fuss"? Charmion replied "Tonight you have royal work to do.

Do not fail" she replied, as the girls both broke into giggles. Being ready, he was led into another tent, where only Cleopatra lay. The maids disrobed him and left. Cleopatra looked him over, then asked him directly, 'Appolodorus will you help your queen? "Standing naked before her, could only whisper, "Yes, my Queen". Cleopatra guided him to her bed, and whispered into his ear, "Lay down beside me, do not remove your blindfold". Of course my Queen" he replied. Cleopatra caressed his body, then looked down at his loins and replied, "I can see you are ready, then do your duty for your queen". Appolodorus moved gently over her, guided only by her breath and hands and made good on her order.

Later that night, with Appolodorus having gone to his own bed, the women lay about on cushions and bedding and chatted about the future for her. Charmion smiled and said "O Cleopatra, you are to be a mother! I am sure of it too. Do you know anything about Caesar? What do you think he's like?" Cleopatra thought for a moment "Oh, lets see, a strong Roman nose, no doubt, maybe thick curly hair, tall. Who cares? He may be fat and bald, but he is Caesar, and I will rule his heart and his country if I have a boy child, while I rule over my empire. This I must do. I know it as surely as I know I am alive".

The ladies continued to fuss over her, giggling about how to please an older man in bed. The next morning, thirty-thousand camels, men, and equipment moved south in one long dusty line, four deep and five kilometers long. It was a long slow journey, with few stops, and as before, done in the cool of the night with the aid of the stars, stopping in the daytime to rest and protect themselves from the sun.

Quick temporary camps were put up each day and on the fifth night Cleopatra, Diogenes and Azar sat in consultation with the desert chiefs. Suddenly, their scout rode up to their tent in haste, jumped off his horse, entered the tent and bowed quickly. He addressed Cleopatra, slightly out of breath, "Hail, O' Queen!" then turning to everyone "I have urgent news!" `Diogenes replied, "Do not hesitate, you may speak". The scout spat out, "Ptolemy's army is on the way using the northern route to come and find you and fight you". Diogenes asked, "Is the Boy King with the army?" to which the scout replied, "No, he is still in Egypt, I was told". Diogenes looked at Cleopatra "My Queen, I was told today that a sandstorm is coming upon us very soon, it may be wise if we use this storm as a cover to go around your brother's army by going southward and head for the Nile.

Cleopatra, with excitement in her voice, gave the order, "Ginnesthoi! Let it be done". Let's move now!"

Her brother's army heads northeastward, was only a few kilometers away as her army moved southwestward. The vast, kilometers wide, sandstorm hit both her army and her brothers' at the same time, blinding them all, preventing either party from seeing each other. The sand was terrible on both man and beast. Both armies had to keep their faces down and covered while urging their camels onward into the sandstorm, many dismounted and held onto their camels tail until they could see clearly. Then finally, her army could see no other army in their way, continued onward.

Her army continued southward, missed entirely by her brother's army. At the Nile River's edge, the vast army finally rested and took in sight of the pyramids in the distance. Cleopatra also looked west while sitting on her camel, said, more to herself than anyone else, "I said I'd be back and here I am". Her sister was nowhere to be found and many of her guards, who were guarding her, lay dead where they fought her brother's army.

47 BC. Fall Time, East Nile River.

The larger boat moved across the delta, pulling a smaller boat behind it,with the Royal Guards on the oars this time, all shrouded in plain clothes. Cleopatra looked radiant, nervous, but ready for what lay ahead for her. As they drew closer to Alexandria, the sun sets low on the horizon, she could see the magnificent lighthouse that beckoned her home and showed her the way to the port and Palace. As the palace came into view, the smells of food greeted her. Gone was the heat of the desert and the smell of thirty-thousand men and camels. A rolled up carpet which had been stashed in the boat waiting for future use, was pulled out by Appolodorus as he then Cleopatra moved into the smaller boat. He then freed the rope tying the smaller boat to the larger boat and rowed for the port entrance. Soon they entered into the Palace's secret water entrance without hindrance.

Docking the boat, they quietly moved down one secret passage into another, with Appolodorus holding the carpet in one hand and Cleopatra's hand with the other as she followed close behind him. The secret passages were pitch black and with no torch to see the way, they had to move slowly. Finally, they arrived on the other side of her palace room's secret door.

Appolodorus and Cleopatra stood face to face, looking a little breathless and excited. Her heart was pounding in her ears as his did. Appolodorus fussed with the carpet, trying to get it flat in the narrow tunnel, ready for Cleopatra to lay on. She quickly adjusted her hair saying breathlessly and, speaking in whispers, "Wait! Give me a moment before I get into that carpet. I need to adjust my dress.

It's been so long to wear something nice. It seemed to take a long time from the boat to here. Was there a problem?" Appolodorus, replied, "No, my Queen" and looking embarrassed "I'm afraid I took a wrong turning. It has been more than a year, and these tunnels are like a labyrinth". "All right", she whispered, "No matter, we've made it this far. You're sure this door comes out behind my chambers"? She asked. "Quite sure", he replied, "I heard Roman voices in there a moment ago, it could only be Caesar in that room". Cleopatra grinned in the dark, "He will not be ready for this! Not in a thousand lifetimes. You know what to do, yes? Try not to unroll me face down please".

Appolodorus, sweating now, "I will do my best, my Queen. I must confess, I am a little nervous."

Cleopatra held his face in her hands, "Loyal Apollodorus. You have been my rock this last year. You've seen me at my absolute worst. From now on, we will be strong...invincible, and your reward will be your freedom". Apollodorus gave a wide smile, and softly whispered. "Oh, thank you, my Queen!". "Now, she said, "First let me

59

peek a look at him before you roll me up. Do I look divine?" "Like Isis herself", he replied, so are you ready?"

Cleopatra nodded wordlessly, then, opened the door a little to peek through and as she did part of her face was illuminated in golden light from the other side of the door, where she saw two men in her chambers, deep in conversation. She carefully closed the door and turned to Appolodorus. "Wrap me up now", she said, "I will offer myself as a surprise package and see the look on his face". As she carefully lay down, Appolodorus, rolled up the carpet. "Can you breath" he asked her? A muffled reply in the affirmative came from the carpet.

Appolodorus, opened the secret door a bit, quickly picked up the carpet, then fully opening the door with his foot, walked brazenly into the room and immediately laid down the carpet behind the men.

Antony and Caesar were studying a map of the city. As the secret door opened Antony saw Appolodorus and reached for his sword and as he did so, Caesar, seeing him look up and also reached for his sword. "What manner of entrance is this!" said Antony. Caesar looked up "What?" Appolodorus bowed very low and cowering, replied "Kind Sirs, please do not kill me! I come on behalf of Cleopatra!" Antony came towards him and while threatening with his sword and said: "Rolled up in that rug maybe?!" "Exactly Sire!" said Appolodorus and as he spoke, he carefully unrolled the carpet, spilling out Cleopatra.

Seeing the woman roll out of the carpet, Caesar laughed and said, "Cleopatra, I assume?" Cleopatra ,smiling demurely lifted her hand towards Caesar "I am Queen Cleopatra, and my home is your home, Uncle Caesar". Caesar could not contain a chuckle as he caught her hand, and helped her stand up. "Very clever, Cleopatra, very clever." he said.

The night was now late. Antony had retired. They both lay on couches, eating a light meal together. Between bites Caesar remarked offhandedly", Your brother and sister are here as well." Cleopatra put down her wine glass and quickly retorted, "They won't give the money back that my father borrowed, I will. They won't give you a boy child, I will". Caesar was caught off guard with her quick offer but looking at her, like his next conquest replied quietly, "Is... that... so". Cleopatra looked at Caesar from the side of her eye, and she drank once again and purred "Yes...it will be so."

Both finished their meal. As Caesar sat on the couch, he started to rub his forehead. Cleopatra watched him for a while then asked, "Are you feeling all right?" Caesar smiled at her, but she could see that something was wrong. "Let me get some rue oil and rub your temples for you".

She got up and soon came back and sitting very close to him started rubbing the oil onto his forehead. As she did so, one strap dropped from her dress, showing off her youthful charms. Cleopatra suddenly got up and asked in a caring voice said "Caesar, are we are not tired?", as she extended a hand He looked into her eyes and replied "Yes, a bit, I suppose...". She took him by the hand to the nearby bed, as her eyes locked onto his face with her heart beating fast. As he sat down on the bed , she stood nearby and slipped off her dress.

His gaze moved from her beating breasts and then downward as she started to remove his tunic. They both lay back onto the bed, satisfaction showed on both faces as she realized her plan was working and he thinking that his dreams had come true and in uniting with her, he was merging with 'Alexander the Great'. And so, they sealed their fates with mutual sighs, deep into the night.

The next morning, early, Caesar and Antony spoke as they ate breakfast alone, as was their habit of doing. Antony took a bite of some fruit and remarked with some humor "Caesar, how well you look this morning, you look like a new man!" Caesar swallowed a piece of his apple and replied "I am...a new man. Alexander has kept his word, she is mine". Antony looked across the table, "So, Egypt is ours?"

"Yes, she ours", Caesar replied, smiling. A few minutes later Cleopatra walked in, wearing fresh clothes and a smile and sat next to Caesar asking, "Did you sleep well my Caesar?" He smiled as he looked into her eyes "extraordinarily well, thanks to you". Cleopatra demurely dropped her gaze and took a bite of his apple replying with a smile, "that's good". Antony looked carefully at them both and kept quiet for once.

A while later, a guard appeared at the door and stated that the rest of the family was waiting for Caesar in the next room. Caesar got up, with Cleopatra behind him, walked into the other room, at the same as time as her brother his two advisers and sister came in from the other side. They were shocked to see Cleopatra behind Caesar. Immediately Arsinoe pushed forward towards Cleopatra but her advisor held her back," What is she doing here ?" She shouted. Caesar minced no words quickly replied, "I have decided that Cleopatra will rule as Queen of Egypt." Arsinoe's face went livid in anger, "I am more popular with the people, she had her chance, and no one will follow her again!" Caesar shook his head and replied, "I have slept on it, and my decision is final".

Ptolemy, standing next to his sister, now twelve years old, sputtered with a quivering voice, "But, but...I am a male, I am now Pharaoh is I not? Cleopatra, standing behind Caesar, said with a smirk, "It's been decided". Both advisors, Achilles and Pothinius, together, shouted, "We must object!" Caesar looked that them all, then to Arsinoe, "You, Arisinoe, will retire, I'll give you Crete to manage. Now I have other matters to deal with, leave us." All retired with angry faces, but for Cleopatra and Antony.

61

Antony looked at the parting party "They will not take that quietly, I fear". Caesar turned to Antony, "Have them followed". Then to Cleopatra, "We have to make your position official, we"ll meet with my other generals and your advisors in two hours. Also, disperse your Arab army". Cleopatra touched his shoulder replying with only a simple "Thank you and yes, I will do so". Then turning to Diogenes, ordered him to pay off her army and disperse them.

A few weeks later, Sapinus came running into the Palace and straight into Cleopatra's bedroom, shouting out "Arsinoe, the boy and their advisors have fled the palace and are gathering an army!" Caesar leapt out of bed, opened the door asking, "Where is their army now?" Sapinus replied, "Some distance off, but a crowd is gathering and throwing stones at the palace walls". Caesar rubbed his head, replying, "Send a hundred men the walls, close all city gates and convene a war council, now!" Later that day, Caesar and his generals convened in the palace dining hall to prepare against the Egyptian hordes who despised the Romans presence and objected to Cleopatra`s leadership. Caesar turned to Sapinus" You are to take some men and burn our ships.

We cannot allow her brother to capture them,they could use them to help bring back their army. Sapinus, grimaced" If we burn our ships, we have no way out". Caesar smiled," a 'trapped rat fights harder.' Reinforcements are on the way but will take several months to get them here. Get going, please, we have much to do".

Arsinoe and her brother had left the palace, and now led the Egyptian army. They attacked Alexandria City and cut off the water supply and the entrance to the harbor to blocked any Roman reinforcements. Antony came into the meeting room and informed all in attendance, "The Egyptians have rebelled!" They are at the Palace gates with Ptolemy and Arsinoe leading them!" Caesar immediately stood up, "Sapinus, take three thousand men and man the walls. Kill anyone who enters". As the men prepared to leave, Cleopatra rushed into the war council room, "Caesar, someone has set your ships on fire, and my great library burns alongside it!

We have to control the fire now! Caesar, grabbed her arms, softly and said" I'm very sorry, I ordered the ships burned to prevent your brother's army from using them, when they return, but it seems that things have gotten out of control, but it's impossible to fight the fire now, we have other things to think about, like your life and ours.

Stay here with Antony, he's in charge here, I'm going to the Great Lighthouse with a few hundred men to stop the hordes from blocking the port, as my reinforcements will need port access."

He then continued, looking at Tuluis, "The rabble has cut off the water supply. Take charge of one thousand men and start digging for fresh water, or we'll die of thirst before the sword!" Tullius got up quickly" Consider it done!" and left the room. Cleopatra turned angrily to Caesar, "What am I to do! Wait here and do what?" Caesar held her tenderly saying, "You must stay within these walls, and be seen to defend your throne. I must now leave. You wanted to be queen, and here is what it means, so stay alive and away from the windows!"

47 BC. Spring, Alexandria City.

After six months of fighting, Egyptian forces were still attacking but with less vigor. Some had climbed the walls of the Palace compounds, and breached the doors but were slaughtered by Roman troops once inside. At the same time, a thousand Roman troops had dug frantically for water and finally found enough to keep them going. Caesar meanwhile had been fighting to keep the harbor open from the Great Light House, but eventually lost control to the Egyptian army, forcing him to flee by ditching his uniform and swimming to the palace under cover of darkness.

During this time, Cleopatra sat in the grand dining hall, now used as the planning room, thinking about which poison would be most effective if capture were imminent. Facing her was Antony, who was pouring over the daily reports. Cleopatra studied him carefully and finally asked him, "We have had so little time to talk other than 'war talk', what exactly is your relationship with Caesar?" Antony looked up and said, "I am Caesars' most trusted friend besides being his general of the Horse Guard, and I know all his little secrets. "He smiled. Cleopatra studied his features.

There was something likable about this soldier she liked. Teasing him, she asked, "like what?" Antony smiled at her, "Well", he said, "he's totally taken with you...and I as well". Cleopatra moved her head sideways and coyly replied, "I see, then I should remember your name then I suppose." Suddenly there was a commotion, the guards snap to attention, the large doors were flung open, and Caesar walked in, very wet and dripping all over the floor. Cleopatra jumped up and called to him, "Caesar! Where have you been... and...you're all wet!"

Caesar did not immediately reply but flung himself down on a chair, picked up her wine glass and finished it off in one gulp. "I was forced to swim back to the palace. We lost control of the lighthouse and port entrance! But...the good news is my reinforcements have gotten through by ship. There was an almighty battle, on the beaches and the Nile River. Your brother was killed, no body was found but his armor was. Your sister was taken captive". Cleopatra`s face went from a smile to a snarl "Kill her now!" she ordered. Caesar took another drink of wine and replied without looking up "No! She is too popular, we have control now. She will go into exile. `and that's that".

46 BC. Royal Barge, Temple of Ramses The Second.

By late summer, the Royal barge was at the end of its two-month journey. To the West the sun set slowly on the horizon. Cleopatra and Caesar sat outside of the 'Temple of Ramses the Second' on one of it's many overturned large stones. It was late into the night, and a huge full moon was coming up in the East as the sun set in the West. Cleopatra gazed at the moon and said, "After all that we have gone through in the past many months, it's amazing we are both still alive! Getting into the palace and meeting you, finally, eluding my brother's army, it sounds like one of your campaigns! I only regret that my library was lost and my sister is still alive and only in exile in the temple of Artemis".

Caesar smiled and replied, "Well, yes the library was a disaster but Antony will provide copies from Greece as a present for your twenty-second birthday. Your sister is better alive than dead, killing her will only bring more problems. Why do you keep rubbing your stomach?" Cleopatra looked into his eyes and replied shyly, "I feel your baby in my womb. It's going to be a boy, I'm sure of it!" "My child...a boy!" he said in surprise. Woman, you are one surprise after another!"

With a smile, saying one thing and meaning another she replied, "We are one now Caesar, one family, one country with one baby but sometimes I do wonder what the Gods have in store for us both?" Caesar looked at her and the setting sun and laughed nervously. "Yes, I wonder as well."

46 BC. Fall Time, Greece, Athens.

In the house of the Greek woman, Dereia, she, Evgengia and Aglea sat around a large table, eating and drinking. Slave servants stood nearby, candles flickered on the table. Dareia laughed,"Well, Caesar has outdone himself, has he not!" Evgenia took a grape and peeled it slowly, "Rome and Egypt, he has paid us back a thousandfold. What next, ladies!?" Aglea put down her cup and in a deadly serious tone replied, "Get rid of Caesar, he controls too much". With that, they raised cups and downed the lot.

The End

Maps

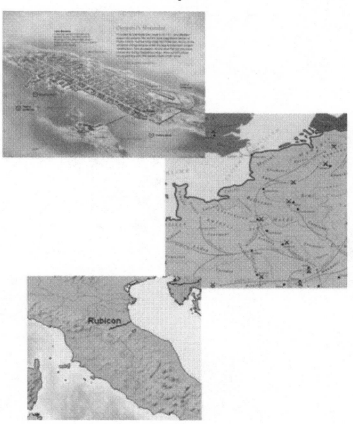

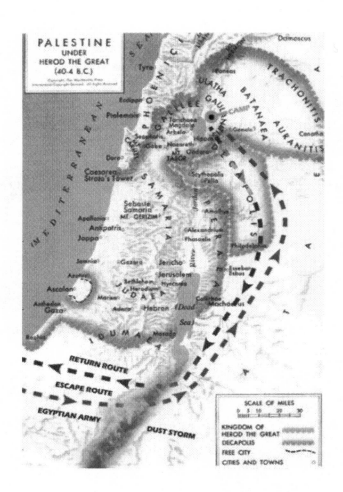

PALESTINE
UNDER
HEROD THE GREAT
(40-4 B.C.)

Copyright, The Westminster Press
International Copyright Secured. All Rights Reserved

Damascus

TRACHONITIS

AURANITIS

BATANAEA

ULATHA

Paneas

GAULANITIS

Tyre

PHOENICIA

GALILEE

DECAPOLIS

Gamala?

Canatha

Ecdippa

Ptolemais

Tarichaea
Magdala
Arbela

Nazareth

Seporis
Cabe

MT. GILBOA

MT. TABOR

Gadara

Dora

Scythopolis
or Pella

MEDITERRANEAN SEA

Caesarea
Strato's Tower

SAMARIA

Sebaste
Samaria
MT. GERIZIM

Amathus

Apollonia

Antipatris

Joppa

Alexandrium

Phasaelis

Jamnia

Gazara

Jericho

Jordan River

Bethlehem

Jerusalem

Hyrcania

Macherus

Azotus

JUDAEA

Herodium

Ascalon

Maresa

Anthedon
Gaza

Adora

Hebron

(Dead

Sea)

IDUMAEA

Masada

Raphia

RETURN ROUTE

ESCAPE ROUTE

EGYPTIAN ARMY

DUST STORM

SCALE OF MILES

0   5   10   20   30

KINGDOM OF
HEROD THE GREAT

DECAPOLIS

FREE CITY

CITIES AND TOWNS

68

Profile

Robert David Simpson is a filmmaker, script writer and book writer.
David has enjoyed living in China, Japan, for over thirty years. He now calls
Victoria, Canada, his home. You can find more about David on Facebook-
"AQ21 Films" or on "YouTube RDS - AQ21".

Made in the USA
San Bernardino,
CA

57982145R00044